NightShade

Also by Craig Alan Hart

The Ballad of Duke Dookums

NightShade

a novel

Craig Alan Hart

Sweatshoppe Publications
Grand Rapids, Michigan

Dedication

To Jacob.

For his direction, encouragement, example, and demonstration that individual thought is the highest accomplishment.

Acknowledgments

I would like to thank the people who made this book possible.

My wife, Beth, should take precedence, here, since she not only sacrificed many hours of my presence so I could actually write this, but spent hours herself proofreading. Thanks, Beth, for caring enough to say, "That makes no sense. Change it!"

My co-worker and former cop, Greg VanderZyl, also deserves my thanks for being willing to answer my questions concerning law enforcement. Alert readers may notice a character in *NightShade* named Gary Vanderweil. Yeah. That's Greg.

My buddy, Paul Brand, and his long-suffering father were instrumental in the completion of this book. I want to thank them for allowing the use of photos from their collections to create the cover art.

Another friend, Chris Heimler, has always been willing to lend a helping hand in the promotional area of my endeavors and this project has been no exception. Thanks, Chris!

Finally, I want to thank Grand Rapids, Michigan for being there and giving me a home for the past 26 years.

Craig Alan Hart
2007

Author's Note

I feel somewhat qualified to write a book set in Grand Rapids, Michigan. I have lived in the area for all but six weeks of my life. As unbelievable as it may seem, I have not yet been able to negotiate a refund for those six weeks, but wish to make up the loss to the city. I hope that this book, in some small way, will assist in that desire.

As you read this book, you may notice that I have broken one of the cardinal rules of writing. Nearly all writing instructors will tell you not to mix viewpoints, for fear of either confusing the reader or making it impossible for them to care a damn about the characters.

The major part of this book is written in first person; however, I found it difficult to entirely impart the necessary information to you, the reader, using that viewpoint alone. Thus, I elected to insert chapters, most of which are shorter than the average, where the viewpoint would switch to the ever-popular god mode: *Omnipresent!* (We hear loud thunder and a bush suddenly bursts into flames.)

Using this technique, I found I was able to preserve the gritty feel of a first-person detective novel and still give the reader a little insight beyond what my main character could provide.

Enjoy!

Prologue

He arrived at the high-rise via cab and, having tipped the driver, made his way to the revolving glass doors at the front of the building. Glancing at his watch, he found he was several minutes early. Damn. His host, who had never liked punctuality, was certainly not fond of early arrivals. A seven o' clock appointment meant 7:05. Not 6:55, 7:00, or 7:10. 7:05. Just another of the old man's eccentricities.

He found a corner chair and sat down to watch the people. Sadly, it did not appear to be a busy time of day and the only person who made an appearance was an elderly woman walking a tiny and ridiculously manicured poodle. The poodle barked at him and he gave it the finger. He was not feeling charitable today.

Another glance at his watch revealed the time as 7:01. He stood up and made his way to the elevator. Even though he walked slow and was stopped twice by people getting on from other floors, he still made it to the 17ᵗʰ floor with two minutes to spare.

He rang the bell.

After a short pause, the door was opened by a short, stocky man with an extremely flat face.

"You're early," the man said, his dry, scratchy voice indicating disapproval. He pointed to a wall clock. The visitor checked it against his own watch and found the clock to be slow.

"It's good to see you, too, Charlie. How about getting me a drink, while we wait?"

"Forget it, Jonny," said the stocky man. "First of all, I ain't your servant."

"And second?"

"Don't call me Charlie." He turned to walk away and motioned for Jonny to follow. "I ain't got all day to wait on you, so you'll just have to take the heat from the old man. You should have known better, anyhow."

They walked down a short hallway and then stopped in front of an immense door crafted of stained oak. He knocked sharply and, upon a command from inside the room, opened the door and pushed the visitor inside. Jonny stepped into the room and looked around.

Whoever had been the interior designer for the penthouse apartment had obviously been enamored with dark colors. Depressed, even. The carpet was dark maroon, with swirling designs of black, myrtle, and a muted gold. The furniture was upholstered in black leather and the few lamps in the room were obviously occupied by bulbs of a very low wattage, indeed.

The only potentially cheerful aspect of the room was a fire in the corner fireplace. It was not a large blaze. Just big enough to provide a crackling sound and a few dancing shadows. Placed in the context of the rest of the room, however, the flames and the shadows they provided were quite sinister.

There was a quiet whirring noise from behind and Jonny turned quickly to see a man in a wheelchair emerge from a dark corner.

"It's been a long time," the old man said. He glanced at his watch. "You're rather punctual. No doubt a bad habit you picked up from prison, which shall soon be remedied. Be seated." He pointed a long, thin finger toward a chair by the fireplace and wheeled himself across from it.

Jonny obeyed the command, although he had no desire to sit near the fire. The old man always had a fire going, no matter what the climate or season. Jonny removed his suit coat and laid it over the arm of the chair. He was impatient to know why he had been summoned, but knew better than to begin a serious discussion with the old man.

They sat quietly for a few moments, while the old man reached to one side, where a few bottles and an ice bucket waited on a small table, and fixed himself a scotch. He sipped meditatively before saying,

"I trust you are the same man now."

"Now?"

"As before prison."

"Have I appeared to change?"

The old man drank and held the mouthful briefly before swallowing. "Impossible to say. You seem a trifle subdued, but that could be normal for a man newly released from confinement. I wouldn't know." Here his voice took on a sardonic tone. "I was never so foolish as to be caught."

The remark angered Jonny and he spoke before thinking. "Oh, but you were! Had you not been the beneficiary of a lousy prosecution, you'd be in prison to this day!"

"I would have loathed prison," the old man said. His calm was infuriating. "But you are correct, Jonathon. I would doubtless have died in prison and the current plan would have been nothing more than a wistful dream."

"Plan?"

The old man nodded. "You have no doubt realized I didn't ask you here simply to take a trip down memory lane. You have worked with me long enough to know that I'm not one for sentimentality."

Jonny nodded. "An admirable trait."

"A necessary one," the old man corrected. "A leader should never become too close to his men. They are merely tools to be used for the greater good. You instinctively understood that, Jonathon, and it made you a valuable asset. Ironically, your willingness to be sacrificed made you indispensable."

"Not quite."

The old man shrugged. "You were the last to go," he said, "which is why you are the last to finish his sentence, with the exception of those poor fools who were unfortunate enough to receive life sentences." He replenished his drink and added a few chips of ice. "I've been a very poor host," he said, raising his glass toward Jonny. "Would you care for a libation?"

Jonny shook his head.

"You no doubt remember the organization in its glory days, do you not?"

Jonny nodded.

"I am not foolish enough to believe I could recapture those days," the old man said, "but I am foolish enough to believe in redemption."

"Redemption?"

"This may come as a surprise to you, Jonathon, but the knowledge of what happened to the Markoski organization, and the thoughts of how I could have avoided it, have haunted me ever since its collapse. To have once been on top of the world, only to become a synonym for failure around the networks, is a humiliation I have been forced to bear. It has eaten away at me ever since the first conviction and, although I personally escaped justice, the responsibility weighed heavily upon me. I decided then that I would not rest until every major player involved in my destruction was destroyed."

"And you're reassembling the organization for this reason?"

Markoski smiled. "Prison has not robbed you of your quick mind, Jonathon. Yes. I am gathering my forces once again to strike at the scum who took us down. Each man has been assigned targets specific to his own case. This will provide the ultimate justice."

Reaching into his pocket, Markoski withdrew a white envelope. "This contains the names of the men you are being assigned to eliminate. The method of the killings will be left up to your discretion, as well as the order and place. The time is also your decision, with one exception. You must complete your list by the date supplied in your envelope. You must also report each killing as it occurs."

Jonny opened the envelope and scanned the names. He recognized most of them: the arresting officer, the presiding judge, the jury foreman.... They were all faces he had conjured up many times while in prison, wishing he could do the very thing he was now being called upon to do. At the bottom of the page was a date: June 22.

"Perhaps you're wondering why I chose that date."

Jonny nodded.

"June 22 was the day that you, the last surviving member of the Markoski organization, was sentenced to ten years in prison."

"A correction," Jonny said. "You were the last surviving member of the organization."

Markoski smiled. "Do I detect a hint of bitterness in your voice, Jonathon? I certainly hope you are harboring no hard feelings toward me. You must know that if I could have done anything to save you the hardships of prison, I would have done so."

A sudden thought occurred to Jonny. "I heard through the grapevine that Matheson died in prison. Who's going to take his targets? And those who received life imprisonment?"

"There are a few lists I will have to hire out," Markoski admitted. "For example, there are a few individuals against whom I hold personal grudges, but I am obviously unable to do justice for myself." He took a sip from his glass. "Any other questions?"

"Just one," Jonny said. "Suppose, hypothetically speaking, one of us decided he didn't wish to be a part of the operation? Would he be able to walk away?"

Markoski laughed as if the question was an insult. "Certainly," he said. "I have no desire to force this on anyone. We are, of course, offering incentives." He reached into his pocket again and tossed another envelope toward Jonny, this one much thicker and heavier.

Jonny knew it was cash without opening it. How much, he could only guess, but it was sure to be substantial.

"You see," Markoski said. "Since we are farming out some of the jobs to hired help, it was only fair to also pay those who sacrificed years of their lives to earn this privilege." Markoski turned his wheel chair toward the fire, taking his glass of scotch with him.

From experience, Jonny knew he was being dismissed. He got up, grabbed his suit coat from the chair, and left without another word.

As he waited for the elevator, he stared at the list and thought back over the conversation with Markoski, particularly the last question he had asked the old man:

"Would any former member of the organization be able to walk away from this deal?"

Jonny doubted it. Anyone who expressed serious doubts about the operation would be dispatched as one of the victims. Markoski couldn't afford leaks.

The money was a pay-off, but not insurance. Markoski wasn't avenging the wrongs to his men, Jonny thought. He was avenging the attack on his own pride. It was a personal matter *and anyone who stood in the way, or even wanted out, would be destroyed.*

Although he was still quite warm from the fireside chat, Jonny shivered. Until he completed the list of chores he had been given, he wouldn't be safe. It was kill or be killed...and Jonny had no desire to die.

Chapter One

"How much longer?"

The question was uttered by my less than long-suffering colleague, Leslie Richards. He was sitting in the passenger seat of my 2006 Mitsubishi Eclipse GT, looking through a pair of binoculars at a house a few blocks away.

"Be patient," I said. "A stakeout has never been known as a thrilling pastime."

"I'm not looking for thrilling," Leslie said, "but if we stay here much longer, I may have to run down to Walgreen's and pick up another box of No-Doze."

"And add it to your expense report, no doubt."

"Certainly." Leslie sighed and took a long drink from an immense mug of coffee. I indicated the beverage.

"You realize what will happen if you spill that on the leather seats, don't you?"

"You'll inflict carnage on my person?"

"Certainly," I said, mimicking Leslie's English accent. Although I wouldn't admit it to my sidekick, for fear of encouraging his whining, I was becoming increasingly fidgety myself. It had been a long day and now, with the sun starting to set, it was becoming more unlikely we'd see any action.

Out of habit, I reached into my pocket for a cigarette and was surprised to find one there. It was old and slightly bent, but would do the trick. I pushed in the lighter and waited for it to heat.

Leslie noticed the action and looked at me quizzically before noticing the cigarette between my fingers. He shook his head and held out his hand.

"I think not, old chap. You're supposed to be quitting."

"Look, I'm just as bored as you are."

Despite my pleas, Leslie reached over and snatched the offending item. He snapped it in two and stuffed it into the empty ash tray. Miffed, I went back to staring out the windshield.

Stakeouts are generally dull, but this one had been particularly uneventful. It was a quiet neighborhood, without even the occasional visions of beauty to observe through our powerful binoculars.

"I have seen not one display of lingerie pass by a window," Leslie said, as if reading my thoughts. "This neighborhood seems populated by exceptionally modest individuals. Closed blinds, drawn curtains...you'd think someone would have pity on us."

"You could always try knocking on a few doors," I suggested. "Maybe a lonely housewife will agree to lessen your suffering by opening the drapes and performing a tango upon the settee."

"You're an odd man," Leslie said, trying to appear revolted by the suggestion, but failing miserably.

"But a resourceful one," I countered brilliantly. "You mean you haven't considered doing that very thing?"

He assumed a condescending expression. "Certainly not! I..."

Just then, there was movement at the house in question. The garage door eased up and I saw the red glow of brake lights. A car appeared a moment later, backed onto the street, and began driving slowly away.

I started the Eclipse and shifted into first. "Dump the coffee," I said.

"What?" Leslie looked at me and then back at the cup of liquid. "It's still over half full."

"Exactly. On the off-chance this becomes a chase, I don't want you spilling that Devil's Brew on me or the interior of my car. Dump it."

Leslie uttered a word that made me suspect he thought little of my cautious behavior and even less of my lack of confidence in his dexterity, but he rolled down the window and poured the coffee onto the street.

By the time he had rolled up the window, I was in third gear, trying to stay far enough away from the target to avoid detection, but close enough to maintain visual contact. The streets were winding and if we were spotted and the suspect was able to lose us for just a moment, we might never find him again. On the other hand, it was a residential neighborhood and I had no desire to use the area as a backdrop for a high-speed chase.

The car turned left onto Lane Avenue, but maintained a steady pace of about 30 mph.

"Perhaps he's headed for the highway," Leslie suggested. "I-196 is not too far away."

"Could be. I hope so, anyway. I don't like trailing him through these neighborhoods. It looks quiet enough now, but the minute he steps on the gas, some kid's going to run out from behind a tree or a parked car."

"Just stay back," Leslie said. "He shouldn't know we're watching him."

As if in answer, the car ahead suddenly braked and pulled off to the curb. I maintained my speed and drove past him. Neither Leslie nor I glanced aside as we passed.

I checked the rearview mirror and saw the suspect's car pull slowly back onto the road. He tucked in behind us, effectively reversing the roles as neatly as if we had rehearsed it.

"That was weird," I said. "What were you saying about him not knowing?"

"Maybe he thought he was holding us up." The suggestion was weak and we both knew it.

"How thoughtful of him." I shifted into fourth and pressed the accelerator. The car behind kept pace with us. "I think he knows."

I checked my speed at 40 mph and backed it down to thirty. The car behind kept perfect distance between us. We passed another row of houses. Several had toys strewn in the front yard. A small bicycle leaned against a tree. I dragged my eyes away from the mirror.

"Keep an eye on him," I said. "I have to watch the road. Let me know if he decides to make a quick turn."

"Well, he's not likely to signal," Leslie said sarcastically. "By the time we turned around and made it back to the corner, he'd be long gone."

"Just watch him. If he's headed for the highway, as you said, we'll have a lot more room to play. Until then, I want to—"

"Watch it!"

The sudden exclamation from Leslie sent my eyes back to the mirror. The following car had put on a sudden burst of speed and was within a second of rear-ending us.

I quickly accelerated and whipped to the side of the street. The attacking vehicle flew by with only inches to spare.

Leslie bounced in his seat, making me glad he wasn't holding a cup of coffee. "Hurry, he's not stopping!"

I pulled back into my lane and began pursuit of the fleeing vehicle, which was by now traveling at least fifty and approaching a four-way stop, with no apparent intention of slowing down. As expected, he blew through the intersection without even tapping the brake. Fortunately, there was no one in sight and I followed right behind him.

Over the next couple of blocks, he continued accelerating and soon we were traveling at almost 60 mph. The winding streets became a slalom course and the cars parallel-parked by the curbs whipped past with frightening velocity.

I was going too fast. As much as I hated the thought of losing my quarry, I knew I had to slow down. I'd continue driving toward the interstate onramp and maybe I could pick him up again there.

I braked hard and brought the car to the still illegal, but much saner pace of thirty-five. The car ahead never slowed and I watched as it easily pulled away from us.

The streetlights were just coming on and I saw two small forms standing under one, tossing a football back and forth. They were blissfully unaware of the madly-speeding vehicle tearing down the street toward them.

One of the boys threw the ball and the other made a jump for it. It was a good throw and almost a great catch, but the ball slipped through the receiver's hands and bounced crazily off the sidewalk and toward the street.

Unthinking, the young boy ran toward the football, which was now rolling slowly into the center of the street. I saw the other boy glance up the road, see the oncoming car, and shout to his playmate.

The scene was unreal. I saw the speeding car, saw the frantic warning scream of the first boy, saw the boy in the street grab the football and hold it triumphantly over his head.

I saw all this, but heard no sound. No sound until the horrible screech of rubber on pavement as the driver slammed on the brakes. The brake lights flashed on and smoke filled the air around the car.

It was too late. Far too late. I watched helplessly as the boy disappeared in front of the car, only to reappear as he bounced off the hood and landed heavily back on the street.

The driver didn't hesitate. The brake lights extinguished, there was a surge of power and he disappeared around the corner.

"That son of a bitch!" I brought the Eclipse to a screeching halt, threw it in neutral, and jumped out of the car. "Go after him," I yelled at Leslie, pointing down the street. "I'll take care of this. He's probably headed for the highway."

Leslie nodded and climbed across the center console into the driver's seat. Within seconds, he had also disappeared around the corner. Grabbing my cell phone from my pocket, I dialed 911.

A screen door slammed and I heard the sound of running footsteps. Looking up, I saw the horrified face of a woman, dressed in bathrobe and slippers.

"911," the operator said. "What is your emergency?"

"What happened?" the woman asked, grabbing my arm. Her eyes were wide and filled with panic and dread. For the first time, I noticed that the boy on the sidewalk was screaming and I pushed the woman toward him.

"Watch him," I said. "I'll take care of this."

The woman tried to peer around me to see what "this" was, but I side-stepped in front of her. It wasn't pretty.

"But that's not my boy," she said, indicating the screaming kid and then pointing toward the street. "*He's* my boy. I have to go to him." She seemed controlled, but her wide, darting eyes told a different story. Her hands were shaking and she appeared on the verge of hysteria.

"What is your emergency?" the operator repeated.

The woman tried to push past me. I grabbed her arm and began guiding her back to the sidewalk. "Please, ma'am, wait just a moment, I—"

"Derrick!"

"911. What is—?"

"I need to report a hit and run." I quickly gave the intersection and hung up.

By now, the surrounding yards were filling with curious neighbors. A few of the men came running up to me. Upon my request, a couple of them helped the increasingly panic-stricken mother to her front porch, where several women joined her. The boy on the sidewalk was still screaming.

Turning, I ran toward the crumpled figure in the street. Once on my knees, I performed a cursory examination, being careful not to move him in any way. He was still alive, but just barely. Blood covered the boy's face and arms and I knew he was probably bleeding internally, as well.

"Hang on, son," I said, holding one limp hand. I was kneeling there, talking quietly, when a paramedic pushed me to one side. I hadn't even heard the sirens. I watched as they loaded the boy onto a gurney, pushed it into the ambulance, and sped away toward Spectrum Hospital.

Leslie reappeared, his face the picture of anger. "I lost him. No, I take that back. I never found him. I went straight to the highway, but if he went that way, he had a lot more power under the hood than we thought, because I put the Eclipse through its paces, but never caught up with him."

"He probably headed toward downtown, instead." I put a hand on Leslie's shoulder. "We made the best guess. It's not your fault."

"Kirk?"

I turned to see Gary Vanderweil, a friend who worked for the Grand Rapids Police Department, approaching. I didn't feel like answering questions, but I knew that's what they needed right now.

"Did you see the accident?"

I nodded. "Yeah. We both did."

I gave a quick statement to Gary. There wasn't much to tell. The facts were simple and, although it had happened quickly, I was able to recall the incident with horrifying clarity.

After a few minutes, Gary closed his notebook and gave me permission to leave. "I've got your number if I need to ask you any more questions," he said. "Now get out of here, you look like hell."

I followed Leslie back to the car. As if knowing I wouldn't feel like driving, he went straight to the driver's side and slid behind the wheel. I opened the passenger door and got in. I paused a moment before closing the door and listened. Although he had long been taken inside from the sidewalk, I could still hear the boy. And he was still screaming.

Chapter Two

I arrived at Spectrum Hospital Butterworth Campus in downtown Grand Rapids promptly at 9:00 a.m. I inquired at the front desk and was given instructions to find the room of the hit and run victim.

The receptionist knew exactly who I was talking about, since the incident had already made it to the local news. As I had driven up the Michigan Street hill toward the hospital, I had listened to an account of it on the local news station, WOOD 1300. I was relieved when the report ended without my name having been mentioned.

As I waited for the elevator, I rubbed my tired eyes. I hadn't slept well the previous night and was really feeling the effects. I had even stooped to drink a cup of strong coffee on my way over, but it hadn't yet kicked in. Maybe I was immune. Just my luck.

The elevator arrived and I got in, pushed the button for my floor, and waited. I arrived at my destination and, after leaving the elevator, stood scanning the wall directory. It told me to go right, so I began walking in that direction, looking at each door number.

At last I found it. Tapping lightly, I poked my head around the corner and saw the woman from the night before, accompanied by a slender, unshaven man. They were sitting at the side of a bed, on which lay the impossibly small form of the young victim.

Both adults glanced up at my knock and looked at me questioningly. I entered, feeling a little self-conscious and a lot foolish.

"I'm Kirk Carter," I said, after an awkward pause. "I was the one who witnessed the…accident last night."

The woman's unsure expression gave way to a grateful smile and she rose from her chair. "I never got a chance to thank you, Mr. Carter, for stopping to help Derrick. Without you, he might have died in the street. At least now…he has a chance." Her eyes welled with fresh tears and she turned away.

The man smiled sympathetically and then came around the bed to shake my hand. "Nice to meet you, Mr. Carter. I'm Derrick's uncle, Bob Croswell. This is Derrick's mother, Mrs. Bertram. Thank you for what you did."

I smiled and nodded, but felt no less uncomfortable. How could I tell these people how I felt? That I couldn't shake the feeling I was partially responsible for the accident? If I hadn't chased the car for even the short distant, if I had simply let him drive away, maybe he wouldn't have been going so fast and, perhaps, could have swerved or stopped in time.

I had conveyed these feelings to Leslie, who had immediately dismissed them.

"You backed away from the chase," he had pointed out. "The jackass just kept going. You couldn't help that. And you can't help your instincts, which were to catch the suspect no matter what it took. You overruled yourself in the heat of the moment. That's not something most people can do, with adrenaline pumping through their veins."

I motioned toward the bed. "How's he doing?"

"The doctor was pretty noncommittal," Croswell said. "He did say that the next 48 hours would be critical. If Derrick can stage a comeback within that time frame, he might have a chance of beating this."

"Derrick's always been a fighter," Mrs. Bertram said through tears. "If any kid could make it, he can."

"Well, listen," I said, "I just wanted to stop by and see how he was doing." I reached into my pocket and handed them my card. "That's my phone number. Call me if you need anything."

Croswell looked at me suspiciously. "You're not a lawyer, are you? Because we—"

I shook my head. "I'm not here on a professional level at all, Mr. Croswell."

He took the card and glanced at it. "A private detective? Say, I think I've heard your name mentioned on the news once or twice. Are you going to find the guy who did this? The police don't seem to have any leads."

"I'll find him, Mr. Croswell," I said. "I have to."

After a quick good-bye, I left the room and returned to the elevator. I knew my departure had been hasty. Worse, I knew the reason for my haste—guilt. Intellectually, I understood there was no way to know for sure if I could have done, or not done, anything to prevent the accident.

It was entirely possibly that the suspect would have fled at high speed even if I had held back in the chase. But the fact there was the chance I could have acted in a manner that would have avoided injury to young Derrick Bertram was enough to make my insides churn at the sight of his small form lying inert on the hospital bed.

I had to tell someone.

The elevator delivered me to the ground floor and I walked quickly outside, breaking into a run once past the revolving doors. Back at my car, I picked up my cell phone and dialed Gary's number.

"Kirk?"

"You and your caller ID."

"It helps me avoid you," Gary said, "but today I felt sorry for you."

"You're all heart."

"That's so true." There was a pause and Gary chuckled. "You must really be bored, because this is the lousiest crank call I've ever gotten from you."

"I didn't get a chance to talk to you about the accident last night," I said finally.

Gary tone immediately sobered. "I remember. Have you heard the latest on the kid?"

"I just came from the hospital. It's not good. According to the doctors, the next 48 hours will be crucial."

"Well, I hope he pulls through," Gary said. "Lucky for him that you were nearby."

I could have been hearing things, but I thought I picked up a hint of suspicion, or even implication, in Gary's voice.

"That's what I wanted to talk about," I said.

"What happened?"

"Leslie and I were on a stake-out. The suspect spotted us and ran. I initially started to engage in the chase, but backed off when I realized the danger. The suspect kept going and Derrick ran out in front of the speeding vehicle."

"Did the suspect try to stop?"

"Intially, yes. But it was too late and, once he knew he had hit the kid, he punched the gas again and was gone. I drove up to the scene and jumped out to see what I could do. Leslie took the car and went in search of the suspect, but he was nowhere to be found."

Gary sighed. "And you feel guilty?"

"Yes." It felt good to admit it, to just say the words. "I feel guilty. Maybe if I had backed off sooner or not even engaged in the chase at all, this wouldn't have happened."

"Maybe. But maybe not. There's no way to know what a nutcase suspect is going to do. Police officers deal with this all the time. They shoot a suspect and are immediately second-guessed by everyone, including themselves. Just last year, there was a similar case, where an officer engaged in a high-speed chase and the suspect ended up crashing into a Walgreen's store, killing two people and injuring another. The pursuing officer felt much the same as you do."

"How did he handle it?"

"To be honest, he couldn't. He's off the force, working construction, last I knew. He was a friend of mine, so I talk with him occasionally and he's still not completely over it. I keep asking him to come back to the force, but it's too painful. One of the victims was a little girl."

"The suspect is the murderer, not the officer."

"Right," Gary said, "but you can see the parallels between your case and his. You did the right thing by backing off the chase. Whether or not doing so sooner would have prevented the accident is guesswork at best and not worth beating yourself up over. The point is, the suspect is an arrogant bastard who was willing to put the well-being of others aside. There's no way you can take responsibility for the actions of those kinds of people."

What Gary was saying made perfect sense and, in the context of the example he had given, I could accept it. Applying that to my own situation and exonerating myself from all culpability was another matter altogether. I whispered a quick prayer for Derrick, both for his sake and mine. It was incredibly selfish, but I needed him to be okay.

"Mind telling me about the suspect?" Gary asked, breaking into my thoughts. "Maybe you can help us find him."

"His name's Nick Gantry. At the moment, I have no idea where he is."

"Gantry…that name sounds familiar."

"It should. He was imprisoned several years ago as a result of the big Markoski takedown. He's only been out a few months."

"And already in trouble?"

"He is now," I said. "All I wanted before was to ask him a few questions."

"How did you know about him being in town and I didn't?"

I couldn't help being a tad smug. "My spies are everywhere. Another advantage of not being bound by bureaucratic red tape."

"I don't wish to know about your detecting methods," Gary said quickly. "I have a sneaking suspicion many of them aren't exactly kosher."

"And you don't want to feel guilty taking information from me," I added.

Gary corrected me. "Or for not arresting you on the spot. I'm serious, Kirk. I don't want to know."

"Point taken. But regardless of how I got the information, Gantry is, or was, in town. Just a few days ago, I was hired to investigate a safe burglary and it looked exactly like Gantry's work. Knowing he was in town, I decided to track him down for questioning. Leslie and I were in the process of staking out his joint when last night's incident began."

"And you don't know where Gantry is now?"

"If I did, I'd be over there beating his brains out," I said, meaning every word.

"Or better yet, calling the police to come pick him up," Gary said pointedly. "Don't take too many liberties, Kirk. Not every officer on the force has taken a shine to you. In fact, there are a couple guys who would like nothing better than to see you stumble and bloody your nose."

"They're simply jealous."

"You've been warned," Gary said. "If you find him, contact me."

"Are you going to return the favor?" I asked. "I'd like to be there when he's taken in."

Gary understood. "I'll let you know," he said.

Chapter Three

Jonny took the list of names from his pocket and spread it out on the desk. All the names were now crossed off and their deaths reported to Markoski. Jonny smiled. Not a bad accomplishment, considering he had yet to pull a trigger or spill a drop of blood.

He had never had any intention of carrying out Markoski's massacre. Instead, he had simply reported a name to Markoski every couple of days, crossing it off the list to avoid forgetting and reporting a name twice.

It was a risk, certainly, but Jonny had not enjoyed prison and had no desire to return. Markoski was the one who should have spent the last ten years behind bars, not Jonny, and all Markoski's talk about how bad it made him feel was utter nonsense. The man had allowed his underlings to crash and burn, and now had the arrogance to expect them to bow to his wishes once again, even if it meant risking a life sentence.

Now he had disappeared, personally checking in with each member via phone to check on their progress. He had left instructions that no one was to try to find him, until the tasks were all completed, at which time he would call them all together. Once again, he was pushing others out in front, letting them take the heat, while he stayed in the background, but still getting exactly what he wanted.

The trouble was, many of the old gang were actually carrying out Markoski's instructions. Jonny had read several accounts in the papers of some of the high-level killings: a police chief, a district attorney, a former judge, and others. So far, the police hadn't put the pieces together, but eventually they would recognize the common denominator.

Well, Jonny was not going to play the fool any longer. The chances of committing...he paused and recounted the names on the list...five murders and getting away with them were slim, indeed. The chances of committing one, however, were much better. And, quite frankly, there was only one person in the world Jonny really wanted to see dead.

He reached into the desk drawer and found a pen. Carefully, he added a name to the bottom of the list.

Chapter Four

I arrived at the office at ten o'clock and was surprised and not a little annoyed to find the doors still locked. My faith in Leslie's ability as a sidekick appeared to be misplaced. Not that it was unusual for him to come in late to work, but I had told him of my intention to visit Derrick that morning and Leslie knew I was expecting him to open the office. Thus far, however, he was completely missing in action, a fact that led me to believe my intrepid sidekick was actually sleeping soundly.

I called his cell phone, left a message on his voicemail, and waited several minutes. Nothing. At last, I abandoned any confidence in wireless technology and punched in the number for Leslie's home phone. It rang six times before the answering machine picked up.

"Hello," it said, Leslie's recorded voice sounding impossibly cheery. "You've reached the residence of Leslie

Richards, world-famous spy and World War I flying ace. Presently, I'm out saving the world from certain destruction, but leave me a message and I'll give you a ring."

After an ear-splitting tone, I began shouting into the phone, hoping he'd be able to hear it through his slumber. Finally, a voice quite different from the recording mumbled,

"What the bloody—"

"You're late."

There was a long pause and I heard muffled banging. "I can't find my alarm clock," Leslie whined. "What time is it?"

"It's after ten. I thought you prided yourself on being able to function on little sleep."

"Little sleep, yes. No sleep, not so much. For your information, I've only been in bed four hours."

"You went to bed at 6 a.m.?"

"Some of us, Carter, have a social life."

"And a business to run. I had to make my own coffee this morning."

"You poor bastard." There was a pause and Leslie's voice perked up a bit. I thought I heard a trace of annoyance. "She's not there, then?"

"Who?"

"Sarah."

"Who's Sarah?"

"Secretary."

"We have a secretary?"

"Met her last night."

I didn't like the sound of this. "You hired a secretary last night? Without consulting me?"

"It was late."

"Ah."

"And candlelit."

"What?"

"She needed a job and I needed to sleep in this morning. At the time, it made perfect sense."

"So where is she?"

"I couldn't say, really." Leslie sounded a bit awkward. "She left here about eight-thirty this morning. I thought she'd be there, by now."

Now it was my turn to pause. "You slept with our secretary?"

"It's not unheard of."

"It is in this office!"

"We weren't at the office, we—"

"Spare me the details, Casanova. Four hours or no, I want to see you down here by eleven. Bring bagels."

I had just dropped the receiver back onto its base when I heard an electronic buzzing sound, notifying me that someone had entered the front office. I straightened my sport coat and brushed the sleeves clean of several unpleasant specks, most of which were quite invisible to the naked eye. If this was our new secretary reporting for duty, I wanted to be donned in a speck-free wardrobe while sending her packing.

I envisioned an ungainly scene, in which I herded the woman from the office, explaining why none of her services were needed. As I'm shutting the door behind her, she turns calmly and brushes my shoulder clean, all the while fixing me with a mocking glance.

I shuddered and double-checked. All appeared well, so I plastered my best "nice to meet you, but my partner's a chump" smile on my face and walked from my private office into the reception room.

Immediately upon entering, my low opinion of Leslie took a decided turn for the better. At the very least, I could feel sorry for the guy. Or was that envy? Regardless, the idiot's taste in women was definitely improving. Sarah was, to put it delicately, yummy.

"Mr. Kirk Carter?'

"Hmm?" Had I been staring? "Ah, yes. Pleased to meet me. I mean, you. Have a seat, Miss..."

"Fletcher. Sarah Fletcher."

"Right. May I call you Sarah?"

"Whatever pleases you, Mr. Carter."

Professionalism... "Fine. Leslie tells me that he hired you last night."

"No, sir. We were mutually attracted to one another."

"No, I mean...as a secretary."

She blushed. "Oh, of course. Yes, he said he had been filling the role, but was needed for more important tasks. Sensitive cases, dangerous stake-outs, and all."

I wondered what the "and all" had been, but decided to move on. There was no telling what wild stories Leslie had told her and I could see no reason to bother unraveling all that now, especially since I had no intention of keeping her in the agency's employ.

"Well, I'm sorry if Leslie misled you, Miss Fletcher...Sarah, but we are not looking for a secretary."

"I can type."

"I don't doubt it."

"And take dictation."

"Impressive."

"Run errands and keep the office clean."

"No."

"Organize the agency's files."

"I..."

Organize files. Now that was a selling point. I thought about the closet in my office, which was at this very moment piled high with cardboard boxes containing all my notes and reports from the past five years of cases. I had always intended to spend a weekend going through all the papers and squirreling them away in alphabetized filing cabinets, but so far that was merely a fond ambition.

Besides, if I sent her away now, not only would I be forced to question my own sanity, but would suggest that Leslie had lied to her simply to get action. As dubious as Leslie's ethics may have been, I had never know him to be a complete cad. More accurately, he was simply a fun-loving chap with a rather loose interpretation of authority. He was not, however, mean-spirited or cruel. And he was right. We could use a secretary and it wasn't as if we couldn't afford one.

"I'll make you a deal," I said.

"I accept."

I was somewhat taken aback by the sudden response and found the girl's willingness more than a little disconcerting. "I'll hire you on a temporary basis for a month," I said, ignoring the highly abbreviated acceptance speech. "At the end of that time, if you prove, for any reason, to be unsuited for the job, I have complete authority to release you with or without advance notice. Agreed?"

"Agreed."

"Now for the awkward part," I said. "What did Leslie promise you in way of salary?"

"We didn't discuss it."

"And yet you reported for the job? You must have taken a real shine to Leslie."

"Mr. Carter—"

"Kirk."

"Mr. Carter, I really need this job."

Her face tensed and a plaintive quality entered her voice. She had the pride to be ashamed to beg, but the good sense to know when she had to. I looked away to save her some embarrassment.

"As I said, I'll give you a chance."

She smiled a little and her shoulders slumped in relief. "Thank you. When do I start?"

"When are you available?"

"Uh...now?"

"Excellent," I said, already planning an early lunch, after which I would return to find my office all neat and tidy. "I have some organizing for you to do."

Leading the way to my office, I showed her the closet full of boxes and described my vision for the system. Cases were to be organized alphabetically and by year, thereby making it easy to find any file at a moment's notice.

"After the papers are filed, I'd like everything entered into the computer database. The program is already installed on the machine at the reception desk, so you'll able to enter information there, while still keeping a close eye on the front door for clients. I'll show you how I want the files cross-referenced once you've straightened this mess out."

The front door buzzed and Leslie's voice, now completely rejuvenated, rang out, "Good morning, good morning!" He popped around the doorframe, his face all smiles. "I come bearing sustenance." He held out his right hand, which clutched a bakery bag.

"Ah, my bagels." I reached out to take the bag.

"No, muffins," Leslie said, pulling the bag away from my grasping fingers. "They were out of bagels."

"I hate muffins," I said angrily. "You know I hate muffins."

"Don't throw a wobbly at me, old man," my partner said. "You called me late in the morning after the breakfast rush. To get fresh bagels, I would have had to wait another half hour and, since you sounded so urgent on the phone, I thought I'd best hurry over."

"How conscientious of you." I turned my back on the offending baked goods and strode behind my desk. Retrieving a single file from the stack, I handed it across to Leslie. "The Chandler case," I said. "If you recall, we were scheduled to meet with Mrs. Chandler first thing this morning. I'm surprised she hasn't called by now."

"You're not coming?"

"No, I thought it best to have someone here until Sarah learns her new job."

"Why don't you go?" Leslie suggested. "I could stay."

"Hardly." I waved him out of the office. "You'll do fine and if you run into any difficulties, just call my cell phone. I might be out getting lunch, since it seems impossible to obtain even a single measly breakfast bagel in this town."

"You're a bitter man."

"Hunger lowers my tolerance for stupidity." I was merciless. "Now, go detect."

Reluctantly, Leslie left the office and I watched out the window until I saw him drive away. I turned back to the new secretary.

"The same goes for you," I said. "I'm going out for an early lunch, but if you need me, you can call my cell phone." I wrote the number on the back of a business card and handed it to her. "Make sure it's an emergency and I expect to see at least a small dent made in the organizing by the time I get back."

Ten minutes later, I was seated comfortably in one of my regular dining spots, the Café Solace. My plans for lunch were quickly abandoned, as a quick peek at my watch revealed a good twenty minutes before serving time. I comforted myself with the Solace Scramble, a breakfast delight made with scrambled eggs, ham, potato, onion, peppers, and cheese.

Just as I was finishing my English muffin, I felt my cell phone begin vibrating in my pocket. Thinking Sarah had probably run into some difficulty, I retrieved the device and flipped it open. It wasn't Sarah.

I stared at the name for a long moment before closing the phone with an emphatic snap. Leaving the remains of my meal on the table, I hurried from the restaurant and strode back to the office, my face set in what must have been a particularly threatening scowl. I know this, because when I burst into the office and Sarah caught sight of my expression, her face tensed and she stood up from the floor where she had been sorting papers into neat, individual stacks.

"I don't recall giving you permission to pass my cell phone number out to strangers," I said without preamble.

Sarah looked stunned. Events were moving a little too fast for her. "I...didn't," she said.

"Oh?" I laughed ruefully and waved my cell phone at her. "Then how is it that I just received a call from someone who isn't supposed to have this number?"

"I gave out your number," she admitted, "but it wasn't to a stranger. She said she was your wife."

"*Ex*-wife!" I corrected. "I'll bet she didn't tell you that! Did it ever occur to you to wonder why my wife wouldn't already have my cell phone number?"

Sarah shook her head. "No...she asked how long I had worked here and I said since this morning. Then she said you had recently changed numbers and she had forgotten it."

"Clever wench." As much as I wanted to blame Sarah, I knew I couldn't. It had been my fault for neglecting to warn her about Brooke. As a new secretary, Sarah had no way of knowing whether or not I was married.

"And you're wearing a ring, so I..."

I glanced down at my left hand. She was right. I was still wearing my wedding band, for whatever reason. Finally, I smiled. "Well, you're observant, anyway. Sorry about my little display."

Sarah returned my smile, with no trace of resentment. "Relationships are great, aren't they?"

I had to laugh at the irony in her voice. Obviously, she had been down a similar road. "Yes, they are," I said. "Too bad I'm not great at relationships."

Just then the phone rang. We looked at one another and Sarah reached over to pick up the receiver. She spoke for a moment and then hung up. I could tell she was trying not to burst into laughter.

"It's the Café Solace," she said. "They want to know if you're planning to come back anytime soon to pay your bill." Then she sobered. "Oh, and I have a message!"

"Not from Brooke, I hope."

"No, it was a highly cryptic message from a Mr. Barbosa."

"*Louie* Barbosa?"

"He didn't leave a first name. Do you know him?"

I couldn't think of any other Barbosas, so I had to assume so. "What's the message?"

"Ah-Nab-Awan Park. Tonight at eleven."

Chapter Five

It isn't that I have some inbred distaste for firearms, but I find the hard, unrelenting barrel of a .45 to be highly uncomfortable and disconcerting. Especially when it is being ground into the small of my back by a nasty little man wearing a ridiculously appropriate trench coat.

"Must you?" I asked, reaching back and pushing the gun to one side. "People might think we're up to something."

"Some things never change," the little man said, depositing the weapon into a shoulder holster. "Your sense of humor still sucks."

"As do your manners." I turned and gazed down at him. His bald head reflected the light from a street lamp a few yards away. "I'm going to assume you didn't leave me a cryptic message asking me to meet you here just to renew an old friendship."

Louie "The Barber" Barbosa had earned his nickname by committing several messy crimes involving razors, none of which I had been so unfortunate as to witness. Sadly, no court had yet been able to prove his guilt to the satisfaction of a jury.

Nevertheless, his reputation preceded him. It was because of this and because I had dealt with him previously that I was now being forced to consider the possibility that I might be losing my mind. How any thinking person could voluntarily put themselves in a position where they would be standing in a dark, lonely park accompanied solely by Louie Barbosa was beyond my comprehension.

"Hardly that," Louie said, glancing around the park to make sure we weren't being observed. There was no one in sight.

I was getting edgy. "Pardon my curiosity," I said, "but would you mind terribly telling me why we're standing here, then? And why are you wearing a trench coat? It's still seventy degrees out."

Louie reached into his shirt pocket and removed a pack of Winstons. Plucking out a cigarette, he lit it, took a single puff, and dropped it onto the grass. He ground it out with his heel and stared at me calmly, unblinking. He smiled.

"What would you say if I told you I had been offered $10,000 to kill you?"

"I'd be offended," I said. "Only $10,000?"

Louie shrugged. "Times are tough. And assassins are a dime-a-dozen."

"Who's your employer?"

"Markoski."

I was disgusted. "What, again? I thought you two had some sort of falling out."

"We had a difference of opinion."

"You've reconciled?"

"For the moment."

"And now he's hired you to send me into the wild blue yonder?"

"You're very perceptive."

My nerves were fraying. It had been a long day and my current situation wasn't helping my peace of mind. I glanced longingly down at Louie's crumpled smoke, but instead dug in my pocket for a Nicorette.

"So tell me," I said. "Why didn't you just come equipped with a silencer and bump me off as I walked over here? It would've been easy enough."

"Ah, this is where things get complicated," Louie said. He cleared his throat and absent-mindedly stroked his goatee. "Markoski paid me a $5,000 retainer, with the understanding that I'd get the other half once the job was complete. He assumed I would be greedy enough to follow the plan."

"Sounds like a safe assumption," I observed.

"And so it was," Louie said. "Until I got an offer for $100,000 to kill Markoski."

I whistled. "Pardon the cliché, but I believe that's called 'thickening the plot.' Let me guess. You figure you can keep the $5,000 retainer and also get the $100,000 for killing Markoski."

Louie nodded.

I stared at the little weasel in disgust. "You're a jerk," I said. "You know that?"

Louie nodded again, obviously unaware that I was making a moral judgment against him.

"But I still fail to see the problem," I said. "What's stopping you from killing me, collecting the other half of that prize, and then going after Markoski?"

"I don't know where he is," Louie said. "I was hoping you could help me track him down."

"You expect me to help you track down a man so you can murder him for money? That would make me an accessory!"

"I'd give you a percentage," the little man offered, exhibiting atypical generosity. "And if you don't help me, I'll kill you."

"I don't like being threatened, Louie."

"Well, I thought it only fair to let you know," he said reasonably. "I'd feel guilty killing you under false pretenses."

I found this last statement to be highly suspect, but chose not to pursue the issue. Also, I had to admit I had few options. Knowing Barbosa, there was no doubt in my mind he meant every word he had said.

"Why me?" I asked. "Why don't you track him down yourself? There would be profit in that, too. You wouldn't even have to forego the other half of the five grand."

Louie gave me a look of intense curiosity, mixed with a little disgust. "You seem eager to croak," he said. "Why all the helpful tips and ideas?"

"I'm just having a difficult time fathoming why you would pass up $5,000," I said. "It's not like you, Louie, and from experience I know there has to be a reason."

"Maybe I'm just getting too old and fat to run after men like Markoski," Louie answered. "Maybe I've finally realized more money isn't always the answer."

We both had a good laugh over that.

"No, seriously," I said, holding my aching sides. "Give me the story."

Louie wiped tears of laughter from his chubby cheeks and blew his nose on a handkerchief of immense proportion. "I told you the first part," he said. "I was offered $10,000 by Markoski to bump you off."

"And you accepted," I accused.

Louie looked sheepish. "I was down to my last grand. I had to do something."

"And working for a living hasn't occurred to you?"

The killer ignored the question. "So I came to town to do just that, but before I could do the job, I was contacted by a third party offering $100,000 for the head of Markoski."

"Head? You're speaking figuratively, I hope?"

"Nah. They really wanted his head."

"And you plan on obliging them?"

"We're talking a hundred large, here, Carter. Do you know what I would do for that?"

"Anything?"

"Exactly. I'm not saying I'd enjoy it. My style is more along the lines of a single pistol shot from a darkened alley, maybe even the occasional hit-and-run. Never beheadings."

Unless you could do it with a razor, I thought. Another thought occurred to me. "How do I know you won't kill me after I've found Markoski and collect the other $5,000, before killing Markoski himself?"

"That's up to you," Louie said. "I won't say it hasn't crossed my mind and if I had the opportunity, well, you never know. But I really don't expect you to be stupid enough to allow that to happen."

"Your faith in me is touching."

"And besides," Louie continued, "I happen to like you. Finding a way to let you live and still make a tidy profit would not only please me, but soothe my conscience."

I was just preparing to offer a commentary on the blatant hypocrisy of this moral code, when there was a sound out in the darkness of the park, a shuffling noise and the muted rattle of aluminum. Louie and I both glanced over to see a homeless man shamble past, a plastic bag full of cans tossed over his slumping shoulder. Louie turned back to me.

"I'll be checking in regularly to find out your progress." His eyes narrowed. "I'm not playing games with you, Carter. I understand you and I go way back, but that won't stop me from cutting you down if I think you're about to stab me in the back. Don't make me do it."

Louie started walking away, but I grabbed his arm. "Hold on a minute, Lou. You still haven't answered my question. Why me?"

The little man sighed and muttered something about finding good help these days. "Look," he said, "I'm too well known to Markoski. I've worked with him before and he's entirely aware of the nasty behavior I'm capable of. He's had me and most of his other former crowd watched ever since he was almost busted. Skittish, you know.

"If I start poking around and asking questions, I'm liable to wind up with a bullet in my back. And that just isn't part of my plan. You've been involved with him before, even had a part in taking him down the first time, but he escaped justice on a technicality. Here's your chance to remedy that."

There was a pause and the little man looked genuinely embarrassed. "Besides," he added, "as I said, I kinda like you and if you help me find Markoski, I won't feel obligated to bump you off."

Louie jerked his arm free of my grasp and walked across the park toward Pearl Street. A minute later he had disappeared from sight. I heard the slight squeak of brakes as a vehicle slowed. A car door slammed, the vehicle accelerated, and Louie was gone.

"Creepy little fellow, isn't he?"

Even though I knew the man was there, the sudden words startled me. "Exceptionally so," I said. "Thanks for sticking close."

"Buggered to help. Even though it is somewhat past my normal bedtime."

I looked over at the bum, who had laid his sack of pop cans on the grass and was glancing at a rather expensive-looking watch. "You'll get over it," I said. "How does it feel to be homeless for the evening?"

"Beastly. Tomorrow, I shall pop down to the shelter and donate my life's savings to those poor blokes."

I grinned. Leslie was famous for having gallant and even downright philanthropic whims. Whims that usually never transpired into anything meaningful or tangible, but his charitable aspirations endeared him to his many friends, nonetheless.

I had met Leslie fifteen years earlier, while in England studying criminal justice as an exchange student. After a year, I returned to America, earned my degree, and set up a private practice in my hometown of Grand Rapids.

Not long after, Leslie appeared at my door, informed me that he had been expelled from the university and demanded to be given a job as my assistant. Having just begun establishing my roots in the business, I wasn't exactly swamped with work and I tried to communicate this to my friend.

Leslie, always the master at grasping the situation and making it work to his advantage, soon observed my meager living conditions and explained the situation to me. His father, a wealthy stockbroker in England, although not thrilled about his son's failure at school, was willing to assist Leslie financially, as long as the young man was involved in some sort of honorable vocation.

Fortunately for us, Mr. Richards harbored a lingering fascination with the work of Ian Fleming and found the idea of his son working as a private detective to be, as Leslie put it, "smashing." Since then, our benefactor had been predictable and generous, allowing us to weather the lean times with little discomfort.

Once business began picking up, I tried to convince Leslie to thank his father and inform him that we were now on the way to fame and fortune and no longer in need of his assistance. Ignoring my guilt, Leslie explained that refusing his father's aid, an act obviously giving the older man no end of personal pleasure, would be a cruel thing to do.

Because our living expenses were now covered by business income, the extra cash was simply deposited into the business account. Although I felt a bit guilty about continuing to accept these donations, I had to admit the growing balance came in handy during emergencies. We owned equipment other small private eye firms could only dream about. Our office, while relatively small, made an undeniable statement to visitors, furthering our reputation in the city.

In short, we were now the wealthiest small detective agency in the region, perhaps the United States. Every couple of months, Leslie would write out a lengthy, doubtlessly embellished report of our escapades and mail them to his father. Because of these epics and due to the fact that Leslie had been made sole beneficiary to his father's estate, the financial future of the Carter Detective Agency seemed assured.

For the first couple of years, most of the operations Leslie and I undertook involved low-profile missing person cases the police wouldn't handle or following the partner of a jealous spouse. Gradually, we began handling cases of greater importance and with each job we completed satisfactorily, our reputation grew.

One such case involved a crime boss from Chicago, Roderick Markoski, who had moved temporarily into town in an attempt to introduce his products to the streets of Grand Rapids. Working in cooperation with the police department, Leslie and I had played a key role in spoiling his plan. The incident had served as a catalyst and prompted a domino effect that eventually resulted in the toppling of Markoski's organization.

Sadly, although he was picked up by police and charged, Markoski had escaped jail time due to a legal technicality and the ineptitude of the prosecution.

Even though not serving any time as a result of the capture, Markoski had never forgotten the role the Carter Detective Agency had played in his defeat and he had sworn to avenge the humiliation. Therefore, it was no surprise to me that my demise was on the schedule.

Leslie looked in the direction Louie had disappeared. "You're telling me you two used to work together?"

"I wouldn't put it that way," I said, shrugging. "He was on the payroll occasionally. I met him through a mutual acquaintance and soon discovered he had information useful in my line of work. Since then, I have used his knowledge of crime to assist in all manner of cases. He's a valuable asset to the business."

"Until he threatened to kill you."

"He's not going to kill me."

"He sounded serious to me!"

I waved a dismissive hand. "If Louie planned to kill me, he would already have done it. Waiting, toying with a victim, just isn't his style. He wants to be able to use the agency resources to find Markoski and make a little extra dough for himself. I've paid him too well for the work he's done for me. He's not going to risk losing that for a lump sum of five grand."

"Why haven't I ever been told about the official agency informant?"

"Louie's quite secretive," I said. "He doesn't mind me sharing information he gives to me, as long as he is kept out of it. In fact, he'd be quite angry if he learned you had the area staked out tonight."

"Ah, yes." Leslie gave me a shrewd look. "Another point of interest. If you trust this Louie so much, why did you insist on having back-up?"

For a moment, I was silent. He had me there. "Just a precaution," I said. "Death threats are serious matters. Believe me, Louie won't double-cross us. We're too valuable to him."

"I still don't like it."

I laughed. "I don't *like* it, either, Leslie, but that's just the way it is. If Markoski is actually serious about carrying out his death threat, and I believe he is, then I'm glad I was informed of this prior to the actual event. Say what you will about Louie, and most of it would be true, he usually has the important facts straight."

"I hope you're right," Leslie said, worry etching his thin, angular face. "If anything serious happens to you, my father might make me start working for a living. He'll never believe I carried out all those amazing feats of detection by myself. As far as he's concerned, you're the James Bond of the American Midwest."

"I'm flattered." I turned and started walking away toward my car.

"Where're you going?"

"Home," I said. "I happen to be exhausted."

Chapter Six

"You did what?"

"I brought Carter in to look for Markoski."

Jonny's hand tightened around the phone as if it was the neck of Louie Barbosa. He wished it was. "You realize that you've put me in a very delicate position. If Carter does, indeed, begin tracking down Markoski, it will become abundantly clear that someone has spilled the proverbial beans. Markoski won't waste any time before searching for the guilty party."

"Let him search," Louie said. "Why would he decide on you? There are no links to you. As far as Markoski knows, you've upheld your end of the killings. He's the one who contracted out the killing of Carter to me and he has no way of knowing you hired me in turn to kill him. You're in the clear."

"I still don't like it," Jonny said. "Why did you not consult me first?"

Louie was frank. *"I knew you'd refuse and if I went ahead with it anyway, you'd have me killed, too."*

"Bastard."

"Quite."

"Why did you bring in Carter, anyway? Are you losing your touch? Can you not find Markoski on your own?"

Louie sighed. *"As I told Carter, I'm too well known to Mr. M. There's a decent possibility he's even having me watched. If I made any threatening moves toward him, it would most likely spell the end of this little mission. Also, Carter's always resented the fact that Markoski escaped prison on a technicality after he worked so hard on the case against him. I knew Carter would be motivated by revenge, cloaked as an earnest desire for justice."*

"How soon can I expect results?"

Louie smiled. He had won. *"Difficult to say. I would imagine I could have something to report within a week, although I will certainly contact you if I learn anything sooner."*

"See that you do."

"Yes, sir."

"And Louie…"

"Sir?"

"Don't ever do anything like this again."

"No, sir."

Jonny hung up and sat down in a large, overstuffed chair. He couldn't relax and was soon pacing the floor. What Louie had said made sense, all right. Carter had a reputation for being a persistent, effective investigator and if anyone could find Markoski, he could.

Louie was also right in saying that it would be difficult to look for Markoski himself. The two men had had dealings in the past and Markoski knew fully what kind of man Louie was. Also, it was a given that Jonny couldn't undertake the task of searching for Markoski. It would be very unwise at this point to attract any unnecessary attention. After all, Jonny wasn't exactly *following Markoski's instructions to the letter and it would only take a bit of rudimentary research to discover this fact.*

Markoski had ordered that no one attempt to find him before the jobs were finished. He had also promised to reunite them after. Jonny knew well this would never happen. Markoski was using all of them to execute his own personal revenge and, once it was over, would most likely disappear forever. Jonny was determined not to let this happen. It was time Markoski paid for something himself.

Chapter Seven

The next morning, I walked into the office to find Sarah already working busily on the files.

"I just realized I forgot to give you a key," I said. "How'd you get in?"

"Leslie let me in before taking off again. He said something about trying to get in to see Mrs. Chandler."

"Any messages?"

"Your wife called again." Sarah sounded sincerely apologetic, so I decided not to shoot her on the spot.

"*Ex*-wife," I reminded her, walking from the reception area into my office and dropping my cell phone onto the desk. "That's an important distinction. Please try to get it right next time."

"Sorry. *Ex*-wife. She left you a message." Sarah followed and handed me a folded piece of paper. I opened it and read the contents.

"She really said all this?"

Sarah shook her head. "No, I cut the really bad stuff out. I take it this wasn't an amiable parting?"

"That's putting it mildly. She got the house, car, and some money in the divorce and she's bitter I'm still in business. It took her about a month to go through the money she was awarded and she's been after me for more ever since."

"You don't make regular payments?"

"No. She opted for a rather hefty lump sum, instead of smaller, regular payments. As I said, she blew the cash in a hurry and is angry at the prospect of having to work for a living."

"How long have you two been divorced?"

"It was final about six months ago. We were separated for about a year before that and married two years before that."

"You two work fast." Immediately after saying so, Sarah flushed and started to apologize, but strangely, I wasn't offended.

"Forget it," I said, waving a hand dismissively. "Honestly, it's just a relief to be out of the situation. Having her call me up every couple of days and leave messages is a damn sight better than smelling her breath every morning."

"Ah, yes. The morning breath. That'll ruin a fantasy, if anything will."

"You speak from experience."

Sarah grimaced. "I was married once for about two weeks. Then I found out my dream guy had another wife living across town."

"Cheeky bastard."

"And a poor one. Neither I nor the other woman knew about each other and we were both ticked off. The sucker didn't have a chance."

"Well, you gotta love happy endings," I said. "At least you don't seem to have sustained any permanent psychological damage from the experience."

"No, I survived. That was several years ago, so I can now look back on the situation with nothing more than a disgust for both him and my naiveté."

I looked at her carefully and guessed her age to be no more than thirty. Probably less. "You must have married young, then, for time to have been so effective."

"Seventeen."

"Your parents okayed this?"

"They divorced when I was twelve," Sarah said, sadness entering her voice for the first time during the discussion. "Strange as it may sound, I think that's one reason why I rushed into marriage. I was so eager for stability that I gave it away."

"I believe that's called irony."

"Well, it sucks."

We both laughed and for a moment, there was a feeling of camaraderie. We shared similar experiences and the act of talking about them had, for the moment, lessened the pain of my own.

Leslie suddenly appeared in my office doorway, even though I hadn't heard the front buzzer. He paused and looked first at me and then at Sarah. The cozy feeling was still in the air and he noticed.

"Well, this is charming," he said, forcing both a smile and cheery tone. "Glad we're all getting along."

I cleared my throat. "Sarah had the unfortunate experience of taking a message from Brooke and I thought that warranted an explanation."

"Ah." The word was both tiny and immense.

I decided a change of subject was in order. "Did you meet with Mrs. Chandler?"

Leslie nodded, his bogus cheerful expression changing to a more authentic version, evidence he was choosing to overlook the present situation, at least for now. "Yes, I saw the old bat. She didn't seem particularly happy to see me, though."

"A woman of class," I said.

Leslie had the grace to offer a simple laugh before moving on. "Actually, she intimated to me that the engagement she was offering warranted nothing less than attention from the 'head honcho.'"

"Head honcho?"

"I quote."

Sarah laughed and raised an eyebrow at me. "So much for your woman of class."

"Women of class don't say 'head honcho'? I'll have you know my mother was a fervent participant in slang."

"Was she class?"

"Absolutely!" I banged my fist on the desktop. "Of course, she smoked cigars and liked to stub them out in her Mason jar of home brew, but that was only when company was present. She always waited until it was just family before she started getting crude."

Sarah grimaced. "I don't think I want to hear the rest of this story."

"Intelligent girl," Leslie said. "Some of them will keep you awake at night."

Again, I commandeered the conversation. "Did Mrs. Chandler agree to divulge any details to the lowly assistant? Or do I have to set up a private meeting with her? Perhaps supply hors d'oeuvres and a string quartet?"

"She finally agreed to speak to me," Leslie said, "but it wouldn't hurt to give her a call, maybe even pay a personal visit. Just to smooth things over."

"Buff out your corrupting influence, in other words."

"Exactly."

"Fine," I said. "Even though it goes against our procedure, I'll do it. What information did she kindly divulge?"

"She and her husband are attending a black tie gala at DeVos Place."

"When?"

"June 22."

I took a quick peek at my calendar. "That would be this Friday. Wait, that's tomorrow!"

"Precisely. Mrs. Chandler is planning to wear a family heirloom, a very expensive diamond necklace, and wants protection for the entire evening until the necklace is placed back into the safe late that night."

"It seems pretty straightforward," I said. "We've had assignments of this nature in the past and have a good reputation. Why is this such a big deal?"

"Because Irene Chandler is a bitch," Sarah said.

Not for the first time, both Leslie and I looked at her.

"You know her?" I asked, surprised.

"I mentioned when I took this job I had secretarial experience. That's where I got it. I was Mrs. Chandler's personal secretary and took care of all her appointments, scheduling, and occasionally even served as verbal punching bag."

"Abusive?"

"Quite. She would get angry over some trifle and turn into a banshee. Then suddenly she'd be a sweet old lady and demand to show me her jewelry collection. Including the necklace in question."

"Is it as costly as it sounds or is Mrs. Chandler simply raising hell over a bauble?"

"No, it's quite a piece," Sarah said. "I'd take pains with it, too, if I was her. But she always has to make a big production out of everything and if the situation is actually significant, then there's no telling what she'll pull. She loves drama."

"You are definitely a fount of knowledge," I said. "Any thoughts on the DaVinci Code?"

Sarah laughed. It was a nice laugh. "That's a little out of my jurisdiction," she said, "but if you ever need to know the best place in town to get your nails done, you need only ask."

"I'll keep that in mind." I turned to Leslie. "As much as this woman annoys me, I'll get in contact with her later today and set up a personal meeting."

Leslie made a face. "Why not just blow her off? We don't need the money, although it promises to be a hefty fee."

I gave Leslie a hard look with just a hint of loathing. "Some of us, old pal, take pride in our work. It's not the money I'm going for, but the name recognition and reputation this will bring to the agency. Mrs. Chandler has connections and if we do a reasonable job, the word will spread. Besides, have you ever thought about what would happen if the money flow ever ran dry? Suppose you and your father have a falling out?"

"Trust me, Carter!" Leslie laughed rigidly. "I will not let that happen."

"Ah, but it could. Besides, I like to actually earn my money."

Leslie bowed. "Touché. Go ahead and bask in your self-sufficient maturity. But don't forget whose money it was that set us up in business in the first place and gave us a much-needed jumpstart. Without it, we'd probably be working out of a studio apartment in a rather unpleasant neighborhood."

He was right, of course, and I was anything but ungrateful. However, I always resented him reminding me how much I owed him and his father. Almost as if he was convinced we would be failures otherwise.

Having been raised on the idea that hard work actually paid off in the end, I couldn't help rebelling against the notion that the success of the Carter Detective Agency was due only to luck. The truth was, I had worked endless hours with little or no sleep to track down jobs and make a buck. Even before the easy money started coming in, I had been making progress and gaining a reputation.

I turned to Sarah and motioned toward the ever-shrinking stack of files. "Better get back to work," I said. "You're doing great, by the way."

She nodded and, grabbing an armful of folders, exited my office.

Leslie leaned over and gently swung the door closed. He just stood there for a moment, not looking at me or speaking. Then—

"What the hell was that?"

"What?" I didn't want to know what he was talking about, although I had a nagging theory.

"You and Sarah. Alone. In your office." His voice was still calm, but now held an edge.

"She works here," I said, feeling a spike in my blood pressure. "Am I not allowed to have a conversation with my own secretary?"

"You weren't talking business."

"No, we weren't. But we weren't making plans for later, either."

Leslie made a sound of derision. Not a snort, exactly, or a hiss, but an expulsion of air through clenching teeth. "I saw you two. I *felt* it."

"It?"

"You know what I'm talking about, Carter. You *connected* with her."

"Is that wrong?"

"It is on that level. She's mine."

"Does she know this?"

Leslie flushed. "Are you saying she slept with me just to do it? Do you realize what you're saying about her?"

"I didn't mean…" Honestly, I hadn't thought of it in that light. "Don't you think you're overacting just a tad? It isn't like we were entangled in passion when you walked in."

"And if I'd been a few minutes later?"

I emitted a short laugh. "Some of us understand the meaning of relationship."

For a moment, I thought he was going to hit me. I would've felt better if he had, actually. It had been a wretched thing to say. But he gathered himself and took a deep breath.

"Look, Carter," he said. "I know you think I was an idiot for spending the night with Sarah, then offering her the job, and...well, everything. I admit it was ill-advised. Stupid, even. And I admit I'm not exactly batting 1.000 when it comes to relationships, but I really like her. Yes, I was jiggered that night, but I really like her."

The sheer desperation on his face caused me to twist on the inside. Poor jerk was falling in love with Sarah. I reached out and whacked his shoulder.

"Sorry," I said. "I understand why you're angry, but you have to believe me when I say we weren't doing anything. Just talking. We both have had some unpleasant marriage experiences, we discussed them, and there was a moment of empathy between us. That's all."

Even as I said it, I had to question my own statement. Was that really all? Or did Leslie have reason to be concerned? Maybe something more than mere friendship *had* happened between me and Sarah. It certainly wasn't what I had been going for.

Leslie just stood there and looked at me for a moment. Finally, he shrugged. "Very well," he said. "I apologize for assuming the worst. I shouldn't be so defensive. To be honest, you were right. We haven't even discussed a...relationship. Likely, that's why I became so agitated. I feel somewhat vulnerable. And that pisses me off."

"Why haven't you discussed this with her? It might help to know exactly how she feels before you make any assumptions. Maybe this caught her off guard as much as it did you."

He wouldn't look me in the eye. "That's why we haven't talked about it. We've actively avoided the topic, actually, due to fear and uncertainty. It's all so awkward and we're both terrified of being rejected. Neither of us wants to bring up the subject."

I didn't say as much, but I wondered how he could possibly know what Sarah was thinking when, by his own admission, they had not conversed. What if she didn't want to talk about it, because she was ashamed of the situation and wanted to dispose of it quietly? Suppose she regretted what had happened and ignoring it was just a lot easier than facing the problem?

"Want to go for food?" Leslie had obviously decided the conversation was over. That was fine with me.

"I'm not hungry," I said. "Besides, I have some private phone calls to make, so how about if you take Sarah out? Stay gone at least half an hour. After that, I'm scheduled to appear on that local radio show on WOOD 1300."

"The Ray and Skip Show?"

"Yeah, that's it."

"Moving up in the world, eh? Who's the subject of the super-secret phone calls? Markoski?"

"Yep."

"What are the chances you'll find him before this Louie character decides to take you out?"

"First of all, Louie's not going to 'take me out.' He's a rough character, but he's not completely ruthless."

"Carter, he's planning to decapitate a man. I call that ruthless."

"I've known Louie a long time."

"Then you know I'm onto something, here. Watch your back, that's all I'm saying."

Although I felt Leslie was being somewhat paranoid, I knew the reason was simply a sincere concern for my well-being, so I couldn't feel too upset about it. "That's what you're here for," I said. "Why else would I keep you around?"

"My charming personality and suave demeanor?"

"Both of which are going to cost you a fortune in child support if you aren't careful." I was still a little miffed about the unauthorized hire, although Sarah was already turning out to be one hell of a secretary.

Leslie was humble. "We'll be back in a bit."

No sooner had the door to the front office closed behind my two employees then I walked to my own desk, picked up my phone, and accessed the private line. I dialed a number and it rang four times. An answering machine picked up.

"Yo," it said. "Leave a message."

beep

I had been through this before. "It's Carter. Pick up, you wank."

There was noisy clicking as the receiver was yanked up. "Carter? What, you need bail money again?"

"As if you could afford it after alimony."

This lively repartee was all part of an odd male-bonding process, a routine made no less strange by the fact that Jackson Wyatt and I were actually good friends. Jackson, a mystery novelist living in Chicago, had spent a year at the Grand Rapids Police Department, before moving to Chicago and spending two years on the force there. Then he was shot in the line of duty and became a liability. Pressure from above and a life-long desire to write took their toll and now he was quickly building a name for himself in the world of fiction.

"I play it safe by marrying the dumb ones," Jackson said chauvinistically. "I paid the last broad off with Monopoly money."

"Deadbeat."

"The deadest."

"Well, listen, pervert, I'm looking for some information."

Jackson made a play to sound hurt. "That's the only reason you ever call," he whined. "Only when you want something."

"It's only fair, since that's the way you treat all your girlfriends," I said. "Consider it just retribution."

"I can't wait to spit on your grave."

"Likewise. So how about it?"

"Fine." Jackson sighed. "What do you need to know?"

"Does the name 'Markoski' mean anything to you?"

I could mentally picture Jackson's startled look and his voice confirmed the image. "*The* Markoski?"

"The one and only."

"Why are you interested in him?"

"It doesn't matter. I need to know where I can find him."

Jackson laughed. "Hey, I'm good, but nobody knows where the M is, except him and maybe his mistress."

"Someone else *has* to know. The guy used to have a huge network all across the country, until the takedown. You don't just walk away from that."

"I can't help you," Jackson said. "For one thing, you're playing with fire and if I help you, I'm liable to get burned as well. Secondly, I don't know where Markoski is holed up."

"Would you tell me if you did?"

"Honestly? I'm not sure. I'd have to hear the price."

"Then tell me this: if *you* wanted to find him, where would you start?"

"First, I'd contact my lawyer and make a will, then I'd shoot myself for even considering something so stupid. I know personally of two other people who have gone out to find Markoski, for either money or prestige."

"And?"

"Let's just say they'll never blow out another birthday candle."

"Okay, so they were careless."

"Listen, Carter, these were professionals. They weren't just a couple of jerks screwing around with something too big for them. They knew what they were doing, they knew the risks, and still they ended up assuming room temperature."

The thought that Leslie might be right after all flashed across my mind and, although I tried to dismiss it, stayed in the background and caused a prickle on my neck.

"It's either Markoski or me, unfortunately, so I really don't have a lot of choice."

"A showdown?"

"Something like that. You remember Louie Barbosa?"

"The Barber?"

"The same. Markoski hired him to kill me for ten grand and paid him a down payment, but before Louie could pull it off, someone hired him to kill Markoski. For a higher price."

"Oh, I get it. Barbosa takes the retainer for your death from Markoski and then kills him to get the higher reward."

"Exactly. And he doesn't even have to worry about retribution for not killing me, because Markoski will be dead."

"Where do you come in?"

"Louie wants me to find Markoski for him."

"He always was a lazy bastard. So what do you get for your help?"

"A few more birthday candles."

Jackson laughed incredulously. "The little weasel actually threatened to kill you?"

"He mentioned it. I can't say I took him seriously, though."

"Maybe you should," Jackson said, sounding remarkably like Leslie. "I've had a run-in or two with Barbosa and from what I remember, he was all about money. Likely, he'll use your expertise and connections to find Markoski, kill you, collect the other half of the money, and then take out Markoski for...how much is he getting paid for Mr. M?"

"A hundred."

"Thou?"

"Yeah."

Jackson whistled. "Congratulations," he said, "you're small fry."

"In this case, I consider that an honor. So how about it, loser? Can you help me out?"

"As I said, I don't know where Markoski is and getting a lead on him could prove to be quite a challenge. How long did Barbosa give you?"

"He just said he'd be checking in regularly. I got the impression he's running low on dough, so I don't expect to be working on this case when I'm old and gray."

"How do you get yourself into these things?" Jackson sounded almost jealous. "Trouble likes you."

"And you like trouble. Come on, what help can you offer?"

"Are you prepared to pay?"

"Have I ever failed to uphold my end of a bargain?"

Jackson ignored the question. "I'm not going to be a lot of help, I'm afraid," he said. "I can do some checking, call in some favors of my own, and get back with you. If you want my advice, I'd try to find out who hired Barbosa to begin with and why."

"Markoski wants me dead for my part in the destruction of his organization. I don't know who has it in for him, although there are plenty of people who could. You don't get to where he is without making enemies."

"Well, find out. If you can find the employer, you may find a motive, which could lead to further contacts and, hopefully, a location. At the very least, it should narrow down your search."

"I'll see what I can nail down. I'm expecting Louie to call me before too long, at which time I can attempt to pry some information out of him. In the meantime, if you hear anything or are able to convince one of your sources to cough something up, give me a call."

Chapter Eight

Roderick Markoski dropped into his wheelchair and leaned his cane against a chair. He was not wheelchair-bound, but too much walking tired him. He cursed the bullet that had caused his injury. The wound had occurred ten years ago during his capture. Had he known he would eventually go free, he would not have attempted to escape. At the time, however, flight had seemed the only option.

Markoski also cursed the officer who had shot him and then wheeled himself up to his desk and opened a file. He smiled when he saw the list of names, many of which were already scratched out. It never ceased to amuse him to see how men would fall into step, especially when offered a bit of incentive.

Although he had never doubted his hold over his men, there had been a nagging fear that prison had changed them.

Made them resentful, perhaps even independent of their former master.

Looking at the list, however, Markoski knew he had worried in vain. In fact, if he had it to do over again, he would not even give them the added motivation of the money. They would probably have agreed to do it for no other reason than to be accepted back into the Markoski family once it was all over.

Old times. That's what they were all looking forward to. The good old days. Markoski smiled. He, for one, had no intention of attempting to recreate the "good old days." Yes, they had been good, but he was old enough and wise enough to know that times change. His time was over. He had risen to the top, true, but it had been a long, hard fall to the bottom.

That was not going to happen again. Once all these vermin were exterminated, he could live out his remaining days in peace. He would take what was left of his money, a considerable amount, and disappear. Switzerland, perhaps, or South America.

It would take those fools some time to realize that he was not going to revive the glory of the past and that they had been manipulated one last time. By then it would be too late. He would be set up in style far away, with a new name, a new mistress, and a new life. A new beginning.

There was a knock on the door. It brought him out of his reverie with a start.

"Yes?"

The door opened slowly and Charlie stuck his head inside. He seemed exceptionally nervous. "There's a telephone call for you, Mr. Markoski."

This was even more startling. "A telephone call? Who knows this number?"

Charlie held up a cell phone. "It came through on my phone, boss."

"And you admitted you knew where I was? That you were here with me?" Markoski's face turned red with anger and,

looking for a weapon, he fumbled in a desk drawer, determined to kill the fool on the spot.

Charlie realized the intent and quickly stammered out an explanation. "They don't know, boss. They left a voicemail saying that, if I knew where to find you, to get the message to you. I just thought I'd pass it along, just in case it was important."

He handed the phone to Markoski, who took it suspiciously. "And how did they know to leave the message on your phone?"

Charlie shrugged, having no intention of admitting he had bragged to several people, mostly beautiful women, that he had been hand-picked to guard the great Markoski. "The only person alive who will know his whereabouts," he had said. To Markoski, he said,

"They probably left the same message on all the others voicemails, too. They won't know which one was the right one."

Markoski pushed a button on the phone and held it up to his ear. After listening for a few minutes, he thoughtfully handed the device back to Charlie.

"It was good you brought this to my attention," he said, "but it's too dangerous for you to have a phone of your own here. If someone managed to discover that you were the link between the outside world and myself, it wouldn't be long before they would discover my whereabouts. Get rid of the phone."

Charlie opened his mouth to protest, but was waved from the room. Markoski wheeled sharply in his chair and went to the secure phone on his desk. He picked up the receiver, but waited until he heard the door close behind Charlie before he began dialing the number left in the voicemail. The connection was made and the phone began ringing.

Charles was a fool, Markoski thought. He had been told to sever all connections with the outside world. A cell phone most certainly qualified as a connection. No matter. He had known from the beginning that Charlie would eventually have to be eliminated. The man knew too much.

For now, though, Markoski needed an assistant. Charlie was perfect for the role. Smart enough to carry out the tasks Markoski assigned to him, but too dumb to be a real threat. Besides, Charlie was like a large, nasty sheep. Given the proper leadership, he'd do anything he was told without even considering subterfuge. The thought of Charlie conspiring made Markoski chuckle.

There was a click as someone answered their phone. "Hello?"

"Roderick Markoski, here," Markoski said. "I understand you have some intriguing news for me?"

Chapter Nine

Taking the pair of headphones offered to me, I placed them gingerly on my head and was pleased to find they were snug, not tight, and reasonably comfortable. Ever since I had accepted the invitation to appear on the Ray and Skip Show, a local talk program on WOOD 1300, a case of nerves had plagued me.

The show was doing a series on vocation, in which various people would guest on the show and talk about their work. The series was somewhat exclusive, of course, since only those jobs deemed of interest to the public were included.

I felt honored to be included in the line-up, which had included the mayor, police chief Harold Dillon, and the city coroner, but was unsure of the radio experience as a whole, having never guested on a live program.

The two hosts quickly put me at ease. Even Ray, whose on-air persona indicated a crusty, sometimes gruff personality, turned out to be a regular guy and my case of nerves began gradually diminishing. By the time the theme music began, I felt ready to handle my side of the conversation.

Turns out, there really wasn't much for me to do. The experienced hosts guided me through the conversation and soon I was actually enjoying myself.

"The phone lines are open," Ray said. "If you have any questions for Grand Rapids' foremost private detective, Mr. Kirk Carter, now's your chance. Pick up the phone right now and call us."

The segment flew by and soon we were in the midst of a commercial break. Ray turned to me.

"I didn't want to ask this on the air," he said, "but does it ever bother you to be referred to as a private dick? Because that always sounded nasty to me."

Across the control board, Skip rolled his eyes. "You'll have to excuse him," he said. "Ray takes every guest in this direction."

"I asked an honest question!" Ray protested. "I've always wondered where that term came from and I thought, being a private...eye, Mr. Carter would know. Geez, Skip. Get the corn cobs outta your ears!"

Just then the phone screener stuck his head inside the studio. "I've got a guy on line three for Mr. Carter."

Ray waved him off. "We go back on the air in sixty seconds," he said. "Put him on then."

"He says it's urgent. And private."

"Let him wait," Ray said, annoyed. "He's just some bunghole who doesn't want to wait his turn." He pointed to a monitor that listed all the incoming calls, along with pertinent information, such as name and reason for calling. "See, look at that. He doesn't even give a topic. Hang up on him."

I squinted at the monitor and the name gave me a jolt. "Maybe I should take this off the air."

"We're on in forty-five seconds," Skip said, pointing at the clock.

"It'll only take a minute."

"We don't *have* a minute!"

I replaced my headphones. "Patch me in," I said. "Hurry!"

Skip pushed a button. "Okay, you're on, but I'm cutting it off in forty seconds."

"Hello, Louie?"

"Carter—"

"What the hell are you doing? I'm on live radio, you idiot!"

"I need to speak to you."

"You're succeeding admirably," I said, angry, but curious. The man sounded positively anxious and anxiety was not generally one of Louie's besetting sins. Sheer indifference was more likely.

"No," he corrected. "I need to speak to you in person."

"Fine. After the show."

"No, that's too long. I need to talk to you now."

I hesitated and looked up to see Skip waving his arms at me. Although I understood how ludicrous the current situation was, I also knew something was wrong with Barbosa. Bad wrong. Louie didn't have a dramatic bone in his body.

"This had better be good," I said. "Where do you want to meet?"

"Somewhere public, but anonymous. We need a place where there are people nearby, but none paying attention to us."

"Well, I'm not driving to the mall," I said facetiously. "How about Veteran's Memorial Park by the public library?"

"In five minutes."

I tore off the headphones and, after offering my profuse apologies to Ray and Skip, ran out of the studio and took the elevator to the ground floor. I didn't like the feel of the situation at all. Not that it was unusual for Louie to request clandestine meetings at short notice. It was, in fact, his *modus operandi.* But the tone of his voice and general attitude were sending me clear warning messages.

I made it to the meeting place in near-perfect time and was pleased to see Louis already there. He was sitting on the ground with his head leaned back against a short pillar, on top of which rested a bronze bust of Henry Wadsworth Longfellow. Louie's legs were crossed and he was holding an opened newspaper, but was obviously more interested in catching a quick nap than keeping up on current events.

Looking quickly around and seeing no one in particular, I walked over to him and sat down on the grass a couple of feet away. He ignored me and continued sitting there, apparently lost in thought.

"You interrupted a very busy schedule," I said finally. "The least you could do is recognize the fact that I came down here. What's the story?"

Still, he didn't answer and, annoyed, I reached over and slapped the newspaper hard, hoping to jerk him awake or startle him into acknowledging my presence.

The newspaper dropped to the grass and I watched in horrified fascination as Louie slowly began collapsing sideways toward me. I jumped up just in time to avoid having him fall into my lap and continued watching as he rolled loosely to one side and thudded to the ground. His head hit the side of the pillar with a hollow crack, but Louie never stirred.

I bent down, thinking maybe he had suffered a heart attack or stroke while waiting for me. A cursory examination revealed nothing so conventional, however, as I discovered the haft of a knife protruding hideously from his back.

I took another quick look around, saw no one, and pulled the knife from the victim's inert form. Wrapping the weapon in a handkerchief I took from the inside pocket of my sport coat, I quickly went through Louie's clothing, hoping to find any information regarding the case at hand. In the inside pocket of his perpetual trench coat, I found several items, none of which seemed to have any bearing on the current situation. I began straightening up, but was halted by a voice at my back.

"Tampering with evidence is severely frowned upon by the authorities."

I jumped and turned to find Leslie standing there, observing the scene with appropriate interest.

"The authorities can frown all they want," I said, "but I have a nagging feeling this might have something to do with Markoski." I inserted the swathed knife into my pocket. "How did you find me so quickly? I just got here?"

"I was in my car listening to the program when they started a new segment without you. They said you had to leave on an emergency, so I called the station and got the screener."

"He knew where I was?"

"Apparently, he listened in on your conversation with Louie. He didn't want to admit it, but I quickly explained the situation to him and he relented."

"Explained the situation?" I said. "The poor kid's ears are probably still ringing."

"Well, the point is, I found you."

"You're a real Boy Scout," I said. "Let's go."

"You're not going to report this to the police?" Leslie gestured toward the body.

I shrugged. "Somebody will find it within ten minutes, probably, and if we don't hurry it up, we'll be discovered along with it. I need neither scandal nor publicity. Move!"

We walked quickly from the park. I glanced back once and, for a fleeting moment, thought I saw Longfellow raise an eyebrow.

Back at HQ, I went into my private office, removed the knife from my pocket, and laid it carefully on my desk. I slowly unwrapped it, being careful not to touch either it or the blood that had stained the handkerchief. Both Leslie and Sarah had followed me. Leslie was standing to one side, keen interest on his face, while observing the tainted blade with distaste.

"Is that what I think it is?"

"Blood? Yes. Very annoying blood."

Leslie chortled. "That's a new one. Care to explain that adjective?"

"Meaning it belongs to the only link to a murder plot. Worse yet, it's my own murder!"

"Ah, yes." Leslie nodded gravely. "That would be somewhat disconcerting. Looking at the situation realistically, though, are you really any worse off now than you were? Louie was hired by Markoski to kill you, true, but he didn't know where Markoski was. What more could he have offered you?"

"That depends on what he was going to tell me at our hasty meeting," I said. "It sounded important."

"Maybe he had gotten a line on Markoski himself," Sarah suggested.

Both Leslie and I looked at her questioningly and then I slowly turned a piercing gaze to my partner. "Uh, Leslie, dear chap, you didn't happen to fill her in on our case details, did you?"

"I...may have told her a few things," Leslie admitted haltingly. "I thought since she was our secretary, she should at least know something about the operation."

"I already explained her duties to her this morning," I said, growing angrier by the moment. "Have you no discretion?"

"Come now, old bean, you're making this very uncomfortable." As usual, Leslie's nonchalant approach to even the most serious of issues disarmed me.

"Well, try to exercise a little discretion in the future, eh?" I turned to Sarah, who was, indeed, looking quite uncomfortable. "Sorry," I said. "Didn't mean to get...loud, there. And, yes, that's a good question. It is possible Louie either found Markoski or got a lead on him. The only reason I doubt it, is because there would be no reason for him to contact me. Louie only came to me in the first place to find Markoski. We weren't partners of any kind, so there was no loyalty. Likely, I would have just heard about Markoski's demise either on the news or through the grapevine."

I bent down to examine the knife, using the tip of a ball point pen to move it from side to side. There were no distinguishing marks that I could see. It was an average-looking knife available at any sporting goods store. The four and a half inch blade was obviously razor sharp and clean, other than the newly-acquired blood stains, but probably retailing for no more than twenty dollars.

I turned the knife over and saw a printed brand name on the blade. It was a long shot, but perhaps...

"See if you can find out what stores in town carry this brand of knife," I said, indicating the marking to Leslie. "Use the phone and computer in the front office and I'll check the knife for prints."

"You're really stepping over the line," Leslie remarked. "If the authorities ever learn you not only disturbed a crime scene, but are tampering with evidence, you can say au revoir to the agency."

"We'll worry about that later," I said. "Just do as you're told."

"What makes you think the knife was purchased around here?"

"Several things. First, it's not exactly a professional's weapon. It's a relatively cheap knife and, if it had been a more expensive model, it wouldn't have been left behind. It has more of a spontaneous feel to it. As if someone picked up the knife just for this purpose."

"That spontaneity could also point to a random killing," Leslie pointed out. "Maybe the murder was completely independent of the whole Markoski scenario."

"That's possible," I admitted, "but it's just too coincidental."

Leslie disappeared into the front office to check on the knife brand, while I set to work dusting the weapon for prints. I found several, some of which appeared to belong to different people. It was difficult to tell for sure, since it's rare to pick up an entire print. All the lifts I got were partials. Hopefully, my contact at the Grand Rapids Police Department, Gary Vanderweil, would be able to run the prints and get me a name.

I picked up the phone and dialed the number for Gary's cell phone. It rang several times before he answered.

"Kirk."

It was just the one word. I recognized both the voice and the serious tone. The former I didn't mind, the latter told me a bad day could soon become much worse.

"Gary. You sound as if a weighty matter is pressing."

"It could be. I was cruising down Library Street about a half hour ago and thought I saw you coming out of Veteran's Memorial Park. I started to stop and say hi, but you seemed to be on a mission, so I decided I'd catch up with you later. Not fifteen minutes after, I hear a report over the radio about a body being found in the park." Gary stopped talking and waited expectantly.

"Are you waiting for me to confess?" I asked, a little facetiously.

"Don't be an ass," Gary said. "I just find it convenient, that's all. Come on, Kirk. I do you favors and you're supposed to be straight with me. What's the story?"

I explained the situation to him, leaving out enough details and names to make it all very confusing.

"So you don't know who this guy is?"

"That I know," I said, thinking the best way to get Gary off my case was to throw him a little meat. "His name is Louie Barbosa, also known as The Barber. He's been involved in some killings and other shady dealings in the past."

"Yeah, I've heard of him."

"Oh, and Gary. You didn't hear any of this from me. I have a few angles I'm working on right now and I need a free hand."

"I understand," he said. "I'll try to keep your name out of it. Might be complicated, but I'll do what I can."

"Try real hard," I said. "This case has a special significance for me." I didn't mention that the "special significance" meant my life. Gary was a great guy and a good friend, but he was still a cop and had certain loyalties. He also had a tendency to be a little over-protective and if he thought my life was in danger, he'd likely insist on helping out. An admirable trait, but not what I needed right now.

If the police learned I had any connection with either the murder or the deceased, they'd hound me until I told them everything I knew. This would, of course, include Markoski and the kill order he had put out on me. With his connections, Markoski would certainly learn the news was out and this would result in two things, neither of which I wanted.

First, Markoski would probably double his efforts to see me dead, in order to keep me from causing him even further trouble. Second, the crime boss would doubtless keep an even lower profile, thereby making him even harder to find.

And finding Markoski was one thing I had to do. It was important enough when Louie first contacted me, but now even more so. Just because Louie was out of the picture did not mean I was safe. In fact, it meant the opposite. Markoski would not call off the hunt simply because his hired gun was dead and, before, at least I knew who was after me. Now, however, I had no way of knowing who Markoski would hire next and the only way to protect myself from future attack was to find Markoski and neutralize him. I definitely didn't want the police there when that happened.

"Kirk?"

It was Gary and I realized I was still holding the phone to my ear. I had been so lost in thought that I had forgotten the conversation.

"Sorry," I said. "Things have been a little crazy here."

"Something I can help with?"

"Actually, there is one thing," I said. "I've got some prints I'd like you to run, if possible."

There was a pause. "I guess I could do that. Do I want to know where they came from?"

"Nope."

"Then I won't ask. If you can get them to me early enough, I could probably have the answer later today. Within a few hours. Tomorrow at the latest. I'll be at the station for the next hour or so doing paperwork."

"Sounds good. I'll have Leslie run them down to you."

"Let me know if there's anything else I can do."

"Sure thing," I said, not meaning the words. I certainly wasn't going to mention this to Gary, but if I didn't find Markoski soon, the only thing he'd be able to do was act as a pallbearer.

Chapter Ten

Later that afternoon, I reluctantly called on Mrs. Chandler to finalize any last minute details and address any concerns she might have related to my perceived rejection of her.

"I just didn't expect to be treated in such a plebian manner," she said, once I had gained an entry into the palatial residence and been seated in a white wicker chair with an impossibly straight back. "A client of my stature should receive the highest regard."

"And so you shall, Mrs. Chandler. I apologize for any oversight that may have occurred."

"*May* have?"

I nodded in deference and she pressed no further.

"This is an important engagement, Mr. Carter. The diamond necklace has been in the Chandler family for more than a hundred years. It belonged to my ancestor in England, Lord

Rothschild Chandler, who received it from a prince in India, while there on an inspection tour for the Crown."

"Fascinating history, Mrs. Chandler. Now, if—"

"I just couldn't bear it if anything were to happen to the necklace, which is why I insisted on meeting with you personally."

"Of course." I took a sip from a ridiculously minute teacup and reached for a ridiculously unfulfilling biscuit. Mrs. Chandler noticed my reach and smiled.

"Succulent, aren't they? I just adore them."

Not wanting to hurt the lady's feelings, I consumed the morsel. It was almost tasteless, save for the slight flavor of cardboard. I drained my teacup and promptly refilled it.

"Any particular reason why you feel you need security tonight, Mrs. Chandler?"

She seemed unwilling to answer for a moment, but finally said, "Well, my husband has received several threats lately."

"Threats? What kind of threats?"

"Nothing serious," she assured me. "He got a letter in the mail a few days ago and we've received a couple of strange phone calls."

"Anything specific?"

"No. They just said he should watch his back and that they would be coming after him." Mrs. Chandler waved her hand dismissively. "It's nothing. My husband was a successful prosecutor for years. It's not unusual to be threatened by criminals who have been put behind bars due to his skill in the courtroom."

"That sounds serious to me, ma'am. Have you notified the police of this?"

She shook her head. "It's nothing, I'm sure. But I thought a little added security for the gala wouldn't be a bad idea, since I was planning to wear the necklace."

"Perhaps we should discuss the details of the operation, Mrs. Chandler."

She brightened. "Ah! Why, yes. The operation. You make it sound so thrilling," she said and danged if she didn't giggle.

Although difficult, I managed to resist her girlish charms.

"It should be purely routine," I said, "but if you want us to protect the diamonds properly, we're going to have to know your entire schedule for the evening. And you'll have to stick with it. No detours or sudden changing of plans."

Although I could have sworn that her lip curled, Mrs. Chandler nodded. "Very well," she said, emitting a tiny sniff. "I shall have a schedule written up and given to you. I must ask, however, that you and your associates remain as inconspicuous as possible."

"We'll do our best."

She smiled wanly. "See that you do. I want the focus to be on the diamond, not your agency."

"I beg your pardon?" I was not at all sure that I liked the implication.

"I know how men in your position think, Mr. Carter. You see this as an opportunity to further your reputation in the community. I simply want to be clear that I expect your full attention to be on protecting the necklace and not on making sure you are noticed while doing so."

"I can assure you, Mrs. Chandler, I—"

The lady cut me off with a wave. It was just as well, since I had been on the verge of lying to her about my intentions. Certainly, I proposed to accomplish the job at hand, but I had to admit to myself that I had thought along the same lines as she. To successfully complete this job would be a coup for the agency, but only if people knew about it.

I nodded and gave Mrs. Chandler a thin smile, saying without warmth, "We'll be discreet."

Leslie met me at the office door with a piece of paper.

"I checked on the brand of that knife you pulled out of Barbosa's back," he said. "There are several stores in town that carry this specific brand." He handed me the paper. "I'm assuming you'll want to check on these as soon as possible."

I nodded. "Did you drop off those prints?"

"I gave them directly to Gary."

"And he hasn't called?"

Leslie shook his head.

"In that case, we might as well follow up on some of these leads while we wait."

We arrived at the first store not fifteen minutes later. Unfortunately, the department manager couldn't remember having sold that type of knife anytime within the last few weeks and a check of the inventory records backed up his memory. The second stop was equally as useless, so my hopes were not high as Leslie and I entered the third sporting goods store and asked to speak to the manager.

The manager, a large, beefy man named Al, turned the knife over in his hands. "Yeah," he said. "Come to think of it, I did sell one of these knives recently. I remember, because this particular brand ain't overly popular with sportsmen, mainly because they're cheap. Might last one trip, but that's about it. In fact, once I sell out this last shipment, I'm not even going to stock them any more."

"Do you remember what the man looked like?"

"Yeah. He wasn't a sportsman, I can tell you that. Looked more like a high-rollin' businessman. Had an expensive-looking suit and flashy tie. Dark, slicked back hair and a wart on his chin. Green eyes, too."

The description sounded familiar, but I couldn't come up with a face. I was surprised by the detail of Al's memory and it made me suspicious. I voiced my concern and Al laughed nervously.

"Just between you, me, and the fencepost," he said, coughing a little and turning only slightly red. "I took pains to remember him just in case I saw him again."

"The quality of the knife?"

Al nodded. "Yeah. I took him for a sucker the minute I seen him and when he asked to see a knife, I immediately thought of them." He raised the hand holding the knife. "I feel kinda bad about it now, but I doubt I'll ever see the man again."

"You may not want to," Leslie said and I gave him a quick elbow to the ribs. Al seemed not to notice.

"Did you notice anything unusual about him?" I asked. "Besides the fact that he obviously knew nothing about sporting goods, I mean."

Al thought for a moment. "Well, when I asked what he planned on using the knife for, he said it was a gift for a nephew."

"Sounds logical."

"Yeah, but when he left the store, I saw him throw the receipt away in the trash can just outside the door. Most people want to save the receipt for a gift just in case it needs to be returned."

"Impressive deduction," I said, almost laughing out loud when Al grinned at the compliment and snapped his suspenders in glee. "How did he pay?"

"Cash."

"So there wouldn't be a credit card record with a name?"

"Nope."

"Yeah, that would've been too easy, I suppose." I handed Al a business card and asked him to call us if the man came back in. His reddened eyes widened as he realized who we were, but he agreed to call us.

"You think that's the guy?" Leslie asked, after we were back in the car on the way to the next stop.

"Who knows? It could be, but then again it could just be an intriguing story."

"Why would the killer buy a knife here in town?"

"Last minute job, maybe? If you unexpectedly need to bump someone off silently and don't have the proper equipment, you have no choice but to buy it. So you go to an out of the way sporting goods store run by a suspicious character named Al, who probably has a record of his own. Did you see his expression when he found out we were privates?"

"He did look rather peaked, come to think of it."

"He looked *guilty.*"

"But why buy a knife so easily identifiable? There are a thousand stores around that sell generic pocketknives that would do the job. Why even risk having it traced?"

"Maybe he was sloppy. Or maybe we just need to find out the answer to that question. There are too many things that don't add up in this little tale."

Leslie and I finished checking the stores on his list, but found nothing of interest. If the story that Al had told us didn't pan out, then the knife was just one more dead end.

Back at the office, I called Gary Vanderweil. "I need you to run a check on an Al..." I referenced Leslie's list. "Baker. He runs a sporting goods store on the south side of town."

"Don't need to," Gary said. "I know Al. We all know Al."

"Why, does he buy you donuts?"

"With a record like his, it couldn't hurt," Gary said good-naturedly, even though my donut quip had been completely uncalled for. "He's got a record to be proud of."

"A felon?"

"Yep. One count of drug possession, one breaking and entering, an armed robbery charge—"

"How does this guy stay on the street?"

"He's got a good lawyer. God knows how he affords the legal counsel he gets. Plus, he's always had something to offer the DA. And he always has money for bail."

"His shop didn't look that busy," I said. "In fact, Leslie and I were the only ones in there at the time."

"He's got a money tree somewhere," Gary agreed, "but his tips are always good, so we haven't asked too many questions."

My mind was whirling, trying to take in the new information, and I stopped speaking for a moment.

"Kirk?"

"Yeah, Gary, I'm here. Thanks for the information."

"Sure thing. But there's more."

"A bonus?"

"I got the prints back."

"And?"

Gary sounded insufferably smug. "Let's just say there's no need to change the subject."

To say I was surprised would not have done my reaction justice. "You don't mean Al."

"Actually…I do."

"Al killed Louie? Somehow that doesn't seem right."

Gary quickly corrected me. "I never said Al killed Louie. I just said his prints were on the knife. That would make sense if, say, the knife had been purchased at his sporting goods store. I had the lab give the knife another going over, just to make sure you guys didn't miss anything."

"We didn't."

"Yeah, so it turned out. There were a few other prints, but they were all much too badly smudged and faint to be of any use. As I said, normally it wouldn't be a big deal to have Al's prints on the knife, since it presumably came from his store. The only reason it might make a difference is because his prints are on top."

"Meaning it's likely he was the last person to use it."

"Meaning he's the last person to leave prints on it. Had the killer used gloves, we would've gotten a similar effect."

"Well, thanks for the information," I said. "I'm thinking I may need to pay another visit to our friend Al."

"Here's another tip," Gary said. "If you want to talk to him while he's still walking around free, you might want to get down there. We're going to pick him up tonight."

"What? That could blow my case!"

Gary sounded genuinely apologetic. "Sorry, Kirk, but I can't conceal evidence of this magnitude. I'll give you time to talk with Al first on one condition."

"I'm afraid to ask."

"Give me the knife."

"Why?"

"Because, you idiot! How can I turn in the prints and the information about Al, without any explanation about where I got the evidence? If I have the knife, I can just say I found it at the crime scene. Nobody will be the wiser and I'll look like a hero. Plus, I'll get to stick it to the detectives, who haven't been overly grand to us beat guys lately. What do you say? I can give you two hours."

"Doesn't sound like I have a lot of choice," I said. "Fine. I'll leave the knife at the office and give my secretary instructions to give it to a large, stupid-looking police officer. Just be sure you actually give me a full two hours. I don't want to get caught in there if some kind of standoff occurs."

Chapter Eleven

I pulled my car into a parking space in front of the sporting goods store and noted with pleasure the absence of any other customer vehicles. The front parking lot was empty, save for a battered Ford pickup that had been there during our earlier visit. I assumed it to be Al's truck.

Even so, once inside I took a quick look around the building, just to eliminate the possibility of pedestrians having dropped in for a quick peek at the fishing lures during their evening stroll. I saw no one.

Al was standing behind the counter when we entered and he looked up, a strange expression crossing his face as he recognized us. He smiled.

"Back so soon? I haven't heard anything else about the knife, if that's what you're here for."

"Actually, I have something a bit more serious to discuss with you, Al my man," I said, as casually as I could. "We pulled some prints off the knife."

Al shrugged. "And mine were on it. Big deal. I sold the damn thing."

"Right. But your prints were the latest."

"That don't meaning nothin'," Al said defensively. "Killer probably used gloves."

The statement caused me to raise a brow. "First of all, it could mean somethin' and, secondly, how did you know the knife was used in a murder?"

"You mentioned it when you were here earlier."

"Nope."

For a man who had just made a serious error in logic, Al remained remarkably calm. "Well, you and your partner just seemed so serious that I assumed it must be a killin'. Otherwise, it wouldn't be such a big deal." He laughed, but it was forced.

Without warning, I reached out and grabbed Al by the collar, pulling him forward until he was leaning over the counter. I put my face a few inches from his.

"Listen, Baker, the police know about this little piece of evidence, so if you have anything to say, you'd better spit it out now. I have contacts in the department, so perhaps I can put in a good word for you. But if you jack with me, I'll see to it that you get the worst possible treatment and sentence."

Al was apparently unaware that I had little power to perform any of these miracles, because he went a shade paler and lost a good deal of his bravado. He raised his hands in a gesture of surrender and tried to speak, but my knuckles were dug too deeply into his throat. I relaxed my grip and let him go. Falling back behind the counter, he spent the next thirty seconds just trying to draw a breath.

"Okay, okay!" he said, once his lungs had refilled with air. "So I held out a little on you earlier. What do you expect? A guy with my record being questioned by a private dick. It can't be good news!"

"Withholding information isn't going to help your case," I said. "Did you kill Louie Barbosa?"

"I never killed nobody! I swear! Especially not Louie. I was fond of the little guy."

"Wait a minute, let me get this straight. You knew Louie Barbosa?"

"Anybody who's done a little time knows Louie. He makes...made...it his business to know everybody. I never knew a guy with as many connections as he had."

"If you didn't kill Louie, then who did?"

Al paused and his eyes got all shifty. I made a sudden move toward him and he squealed and jumped back. "Lay off! I don't know who killed him!"

"Why are you so nervous, Al? It's a cinch you're not jumpy just because you sold a knife that ended up being used in a murder. You know something."

Leslie stepped forward. "Better speak up, old man. Both Kirk and I personally know the officer who's coming here to arrest you. If we're not around to put in a good word for you, it might be a long ride to the station. A very long ride, indeed."

Leslie sounded so ominous that I half-believed him myself, even though the idea of Gary being abusive to anyone, much less a mere suspect, was laughable. Al, however, was not acquainted with the officer in question and Leslie was quite convincing. Again, he raised his hands toward us, palms out in an attitude of submission.

"All right, all right. I admit I lied to you guys earlier when you came in. I made up that story about the guy buyin' the knife for his nephew."

"Pretty elaborate tale," I said. "Why not just deny ever seeing the knife before?"

"I have more of them in stock," Al said. "If I said I'd never seen 'em and the cops found 'em in the store, I'd look bad."

"But why go through such lengths?" Leslie asked. "You could have simply said you sold this type of knife, but didn't remember selling one lately. That's what all the other shop owners said. You would have fit right in. Why make yourself stand out by telling a detailed account of the sale?"

"I was worried about the fingerprints," Al admitted. "I work the store myself and so I stock all the inventory. Those knives don't come in cases, so it was a cinch my prints would be on it."

I shrugged. "The police would make allowance for that."

"Guys like me don't get the benefit of the doubt," Al said with a rueful laugh. "I thought maybe if I told a story like the one I gave you guys, the cops would assume I was comin' clean."

"It was a good attempt," I said. "I'll give you that."

I had to give Al some credit. In his shoes, I might have done the same thing. Having a long record as he did, it was sometimes difficult to get fair treatment from the authorities. Innocent until proven guilty didn't always apply to those already convicted of other crimes. They were easy targets. If he had simply denied knowing anything about the knife, it would have immediately cast him under suspicion, especially after his fingerprints were discovered.

The only place where Al's logic broke down was his failure to maintain his original story. Had I not managed to scare him into contradicting himself and making the fatal slip of the tongue, he might have been able to stick to the story and slip through the cracks. Fortunately for me, Al was a coward.

"Well, I feel we're coming to an understanding," I said genially. "Now, how about telling us the real story?"

Al looked around nervously. "Can you really make it easy on me with the cops?"

"I'll do what I can," I said. The man's piteous attitude was making me feel a bit guilty about my grandiose claims. It wasn't likely I'd have much influence over his treatment and would be powerless to affect the ultimate outcome of his case.

"When are they comin'?"

I glanced at my watch. "You've got about an hour. Better speak fast."

Al nodded and walked quickly to the front door, where he locked it and then propped a "Closed" sign against the front window.

"Come on back to my office," he said. "I'll tell you all about it."

Leslie and I followed the big man into the back of the store and into a tiny room occupied by a chaotic desk, stacks of boxes, one desk chair, and a suspicious folding chair that leaned dejectedly against a swaying floor lamp. The room was darkly lit and smelled of Redman chewing tobacco.

Al walked behind the desk and plopped into the chair. I waited expectantly for it to collapse under his wait, but the chair was determined and survived the onslaught. I motioned to Leslie to take the folding chair, but he was wearing a new pair of pants and backed away. He found a sturdy box, brushed off the dust, and sat down.

Having no alternative, I set up the folding chair and positioned myself at an angle, so I could watch both Al and the office door. Al opened a desk drawer and reached in with his right hand. He glanced up to find my 9mm Glock 19 staring him in the eyes.

"Not so fast, Al," I said coolly. "I can't miss from this distance."

A few beads of sweat appeared on Al's forehead and he used his left hand to wipe them away. "Relax," he said shakily. "Didn't mean to startle you. I was just going for a chew."

"Make it slow."

Following my instructions, Al carefully withdrew a round tin of tobacco. I had been wrong. It was Skoal.

After he had inserted a liberal pinch into his cheek, he leaned back in his chair and looked at Leslie and me with an expression of both fear and cunning. As spinelessly as Al had behaved in the store, I didn't trust the man. He had needlessly sabotaged his own alibi, but I was getting a sense that he had not yet surrendered to the inevitable. He knew the police would be there within the hour to take him in and, likely, hold him for suspicion in the killing of Louie Barbosa. If there's one thing Al didn't need right now, it was a murder rap.

"Part of what I said was true," Al began. "I didn't kill Barbosa and I did sell the knife to a man who came in the store yesterday."

"Did you know the man?"

"I'd met him before."

"And did you know why he was purchasing the knife?"

"I had my suspicions."

"Why did you suspect?"

Al spit some tobacco juice into a crusty glass that sat on the desk. To my horror, I saw it was already half-full of the same. I shuddered. Al wasn't answering my question.

"Why did you suspect?" I repeated.

"I'm not sure I can tell this story in less than an hour," Al said. "I'm not even sure I should tell it at all."

"I'm going to guarantee that you should," I said. "Proceed."

I could see Al wasn't at all sure I was in any position to guarantee such a thing. Actually, I wasn't, but I was counting on Al's fear and desire to escape serious trouble to bail me out. Finally, he began.

"Have you ever heard of a man named Roderick Markoski?"

"Yes, I believe his name was mentioned in the papers a few years back," I said vaguely.

"It was more than mentioned," Al said. "It was headline stuff. The guy used to have a huge crime ring in a bunch of big cites, like Chicago, New York, Detroit, and others. He also had joints in smaller bergs like Grand Rapids. In some ways, he liked it better that way. Not as much suspicion, not as many cops…let's face it, not many people expect places like Grand Rapids to be a home to mob types. Part of his front was a chain of sporting goods stores."

"This being one of them?" I interrupted.

"Yeah." Al paused for a spit and then continued. "Anyway, about ten years ago, Markoski's ring was broke up by a wave of cop raids and single arrests. A lot of people were in on the takedowns, but most people figured that it all began because of an inside leak. That's about the only way some of these rings can be busted.

"Over the past couple of years, most of the guys arrested have been getting released. Either they served their time or it's a parole deal. Either way, with the exception of the lifers, most of the old Markoski gang is showin' up back on the streets."

"Does that include you?"

Al nodded. "I did a couple of years because of the Markoski fall. I've been out for awhile, now, but it wasn't until a few weeks ago that I was contacted by the boss himself."

"Markoski?"

Again, Al nodded, enjoying the looks of surprise on our faces. "I was shocked, too. The old man was still the same. Kinda snobbish, if you know what I mean. He still takes it for granted that everybody's goin' to hop to his every command."

"He's giving orders?"

"Big orders. He's been sendin' out lists to everyone who was taken down."

"Lists of what?"

"Names. Names of people who were involved in the destruction of the Markoski gang."

"What are the lists for?"

"They're death warrants. Markoski wants everyone who gets a list to take out every person mentioned."

"And they're doing it?"

"So far. You gotta understand the hold Markoski has over these people. They're used to obeyin' his demands. The old man also offered some incentives." Al again reached into the desk drawer and this time pulled out a thick manila envelope. He opened the flap and shook the envelope to allow several tightly stacked sheaves of bills to fall onto the desk surface.

"That's quite an incentive," I said finally.

"Fifty thousand dollars worth, to be exact," Al said.

"I take it you've received one of these lists?"

Al nodded. "Yeah, I got one. I haven't acted on it, yet. And I don't intend to. Like I said, I can't afford to go down for murder. Not with my record, especially. I'd be inside for the rest of my life."

The room was hot and stuffy. I reached into my pocket and my fingers closed over a stray cigarette. I pulled it out and was about to ask Al for a light, when Leslie jerked the smoke away from me and ground it out on the concrete floor. I scowled at him, but let it go and turned back to Al.

"I take it you can't just send the money back? Maybe say, 'thanks, but no thanks'?"

Al laughed. "If only it was that easy. I said there were incentives. That was the first."

"And the second?"

"Markoski never said this outright," Al said, "but we all know him and if we stab him in the back, it won't be long before we find our own names on a list."

"So what are you going to do?" I asked. "Surely Markoski will notice if you keep the money, but don't carry out his wishes."

"It would get back to him," Al said sarcastically. "Anyway, a few days ago, a guy came in and asked about a knife. We recognized each other right off as having been part of the old Markoski group. He said he just wanted a cheap one, as generic as I had. Knowing about the lists and seeing how nervous the guy was, I had a sneakin' suspicion about how the knife was going to be used. Then I heard the news about Barbosa."

"Is it possible the man who purchased the knife came here on purpose?"

"To buy the knife, you mean? Yeah, it's possible. In fact, it's likely. Most of the gang knew about the sporting goods stores and even where they were. The stores were used as meeting places, drop-off locations, and the storage of illegal stuff."

"Drugs?"

Al nodded. "Drugs, weapons, you name it. This guy probably came in here to buy the knife, knowing I would also be involved in the operation and, because of that, keep quiet when news of the murder came out."

"So what are your plans now?"

"I've been in contact with someone else of the old gang, just outta prison, who has no wish to go back. He's plannin' to take Markoski out. That's the only way out for those of us who don't want to do the dirty work."

"So it's a kill or be killed situation?"

"Yep. We don't have no choice."

"Who's the other conspirator?"

"That I ain't gonna say," Al said, shaking his head. "If one of us goes down, the other won't be long in joinin' him."

"Why not just go to the police with what you know?"

Al was horrified. "I wouldn't last a week! Markoski has contacts there, too. Besides, the old man has disappeared and no one knows where he is. If the cops start poking around, Markoski will know. From there, it would be a simple matter to find out who's not doing their share and that will tell him who ratted on him. Then we're toast."

"Don't think I'm ungrateful, Al," I said, shifting in my seat. The folding chair groaned ominously and I quickly stopped shifting. "But I'm really at a loss as to why you are telling us all this."

"You said you could make it easier on me with the cops. If I'm gonna help take out Markoski, I need to be out of jail, don't I?"

"It would help," I said, glancing at my watch. We only had about fifteen minutes. "What makes you think I won't tell the police what you've told me?"

Al smiled craftily at me. "You haven't yet."

"Meaning?"

"The other guy I mentioned, the one who's plannin' to stub out Mr. M? He's the one who hired Barbosa to kill Markoski. Gave Barbosa the money Markoski gave him, in fact. Then Barbosa told you about the plan and you haven't spilled the beans yet. That makes me think that you probably won't.

"And it's like Barbosa told my friend, we don't want to do the pokin' around if we can help it. That would be almost as bad as the cops doin' it. Markoski knows some of the guys won't take well to bein' ordered around like this, especially not after just getting outta prison. That's why he's gone into hidin'."

"And I'm on one of the lists."

"You're on *the* list," Al said. "Markoski has a personal list of people he wants killed and you're on it. As you might know, he's in a wheelchair a lot of the time after being shot by a cop during the arrest, so he obviously can't carry out the killings. He's hiring them out and Barbosa was one of the hitmen."

"Assigned to me."

"Bingo."

"You know, Al, I said this to Barbosa and I'll say it to you. I don't really like being made an accessory in all this."

"We aren't the ones who done it," Al said. "Markoski dragged you into the mess by orderin' you dead. Now it's your turn to do somethin' about it. Just remember, the police are off limits. Mr. M has people in there who report back to him. That includes the GRPD."

"I find that hard to believe. I know a lot of those guys."

"You can believe it or not, but it's true. Don't tell them nothin'. If you do, you've endangered us all and I'll take you out myself. Remember Louie? He planned to double-cross Markoski and now he's dead. You can see how fast the man can work."

At that moment, Al looked nothing like the whiny, scared man he'd been earlier. It wasn't until now that I fully realized the seriousness of the issue. It had been obvious from the beginning, but it hadn't dawned on me. Someone was out to kill me and they were serious about it.

"Was your co-conspirator the one who hired Louie to take out Markoski?"

Al nodded. "Yeah. Obviously, that didn't go so well. Markoski's more well-informed than we even thought. We still don't know how he found out about that."

A sudden thought occurred to me. "If he knew about Louie telling me, then he certainly knows that I know. Which makes me even more of a target."

"That's about the size of it," Al said. "Like it or not, you're involved. The best thing for you to do is throw in with us and find Markoski before he finds out what we're up to."

I looked at my watch and saw it was time to go. I stood up and Leslie followed my lead.

"One more thing," I said. "You said you immediately recognized the man who came in to buy the knife. Who was it?"

Al balked and I thought for a moment he was going to clam up. Then he shrugged and threw his hands up in a helpless gesture.

"Oh, what the hell," he said. "I've already spilled my guts to you guys. Maybe if you can get the guy, it'll tie up a loose end for me. His name's Nick Gantry."

Chapter Twelve

"Hello, the Carter Detective Agency. How may I help you?"

"Yes..." Jonny paused for a moment and quickly rethought the phone call. Perhaps contacting Carter wasn't the greatest idea. On the other hand, time was winding down and Jonny needed any help possible in tracking down his target. Markoski had hidden well. Besides, if Markoski had found out that Carter was in on the hunt, it would move him up on the schedule. He'd need to know.

"How may I help you?" the agency's secretary asked again.

"Mr. Carter, please."

"I'm sorry, he's not available right now. May I take a message?"

"This is Jonathon Buschetti. Tell him I have information about a recent murder and future one as well."

"I'm afraid I'll need a little more information than that, Mr...Buschetti, was it?"

"Yes."

"Mr. Carter's a very busy man."

"Just give him the message," Jonny said. "Tell him it involves an old enemy. He should know what that means."

The secretary sighed. "Mr. Buschetti, I...oh, Mr. Carter just walked in. One moment."

It was more than one moment, but eventually a man's voice spoke. "Mr. Buschetti?"

"Yes. Is this Carter?"

"Yes, it is. What is this all about?"

"Do you remember Roderick Markoski?"

"Very well."

"I understand you had recent dealings with a Louie Barbosa."

"Who?"

Jonny chuckled. "Let's not be coy, Mr. Carter. I know all about your deal with Louie."

"It was hardly a deal," Carter said. "He threatened to kill me."

"He always was a bit melodramatic."

"Was? So you know he has been—"

"Murdered, yes. I just heard. As he may have told you, Mr. Carter, I am the one who hired him to kill Markoski."

"No, he was suitably vague. No names."

"Well, no matter. The situation is dire, Mr. Carter, and that is why I am calling."

"I assumed when Louie was murdered that it had something to do with Markoski."

"Somehow he knew that Louie had turned on him. Markoski never wastes time in those situations."

"Not to disagree or seem disrespectful to Louie's memory," Carter said, "but why have you contacted me? It seems you would be heading for the hills. If Markoski knew about Louie, then he may have known about you."

"No, I doubt that. The only person who knew about me was Louie...and he won't tell."

"Perhaps he told before he was killed."

Jonny considered this. "Have you seen the body?"

"Yes. I found it."

"Then you know he wasn't tortured beforehand."

"Nothing obvious, no. It was a simple knife wound to the back."

"Then I doubt Markoski has any news of me. If Louie didn't even tell you about me when he brought you into this, then I doubt he told anyone else. Louie was always careful not to get close to anyone."

"Back to the question," Carter said. "Why have you contacted me?"

"I still want you on the job," Jonny replied. "I need all the help I can get to track Markoski down. If you hear anything, contact me. I also wanted to mention that it's possible Markoski knows you were in cahoots with Louie. If that's the case, the kill order on you has doubtless been made a higher priority. As I said, Markoski never wastes time in these situations."

"So you're saying that finding Markoski is also in my best interest?"

"It certainly is. We both have something to gain by finding him, Mr. Carter. I to kill, you to keep from being killed."

Chapter Thirteen

After the conversation with Jonny Buschetti, I hung up the phone feeling not a little creeped out. Things were moving quickly, too quickly. I hadn't asked for any of this, but here I was, right in the thick of it. I turned to Sarah.

"What are you doing still here, by the way? It's late. Did I forget to mention that I don't pay overtime?"

She started to laugh, but it was interrupted by a yawn of monumental proportions. "Sorry. I got into a groove and didn't want to stop my momentum." She looked at the wall clock. It was eight o'clock. "I didn't realize it was so late."

"How did you get here this morning?" I asked. "Did you drive?"

"No, I took the bus."

"Come on," I said. "I'll drive you home."

Sarah relented without argument, gathered her belongings, and we exited the office. I flipped the light switch and closed the main door, locking it behind me. I had an extra key on the ring, so I slid it off and handed it to Sarah.

"I'd better give you this while I'm thinking about it," I said. "Now you won't have to rely on the punctuality of a couple single males."

Once in the car, I shifted into gear and was preparing to drive out onto the street when I suddenly realized that I didn't know where Sarah lived. Upon my request for directions, she steered me to a Motel 6 on the outskirts of town.

"You live in a motel?"

"Just until I save up some money," she said. "Then I plan on renting an apartment. Would you like to come in for a cup of coffee?"

"I'm not a big fan of coffee," I said, "but if you have any other breed of liquid refreshment…"

"I think I have some Coke."

We exited the car and walked to her room. She fished in her purse to find the key card, brought it out, and opened the door.

"Have you ever noticed that hotel rooms have a distinct smell?" I said. "I think it's a law."

Sarah laughed and turned on a small coffee maker. "Could be. They have laws for much stupider things." She grabbed a Styrofoam cup and poured some Coke into it. "Sorry, I don't have ice and all my glasses are in storage."

I accepted the offering. "I like casual."

"Good, me too." Sarah kicked off her shoes and dropped onto the bed with a sigh. "I didn't realize I had been working so hard," she said, massaging the back her neck. "That's quite a project you started me off with."

"I admit it's daunting," I said. "Why do you think I haven't tackled it? You're doing a great job, though."

"I've always been good at organization. I guess I have a logical mind."

"That can be both a blessing and a curse."

"I guess a private detective would have to have a logical mind. Do you and Leslie work well together?"

I was surprised by the question. "Yes, I guess so. We have our disagreements, but as long as he does what I tell him, everything's fine." I laughed to let her know I was just kidding, but I needn't have bothered. Sarah was a quick study.

"Well, you are the boss, after all." She got up to get a cup of coffee. "Speaking of Leslie...has he mentioned anything about me?"

"Like what?"

"Anything. Well, about us."

"Us? You and Leslie?"

"Yes."

This was not a conversation I wanted to have, but I couldn't devise a quick, painless way to avoid it. "We talked a little about it," I admitted. "He said you two hadn't, though. I think that was his main concern."

"It's mine, too," Sarah said. "I think Leslie's under the impression that we have a future together."

"And you don't?"

Sarah shook her head. "I know what you're thinking, Kirk. That night with Leslie was an aberration brought about by moonlight, alcohol, and loneliness. I don't usually pick up strange men. I'm more about relationships."

"Well, in your own defense, I'd have to say that no matter what kind of relationship you had with Leslie, he'd still be a strange man."

Sarah grinned. "You speak the truth. But he's a sweet guy. I don't want to hurt him, but I know there isn't a future for us, either."

I was still standing near the door, unsure of where to park myself. There wasn't much furniture in the room and the only chair had Sarah's belongings piled on it. She noticed and motioned toward the bed.

"Sorry about the mess," she said. "Go ahead and have a seat there. I'll only be a minute." She added cream and sugar to her coffee and then came over and sat down next to me. "What about you, Kirk?"

"I don't pick up strange men, either."

"No, silly. Are you soured on relationships or are you still open?"

"That depends."

"On?"

"On the relationship."

"So you're still open."

I shrugged, getting more uncomfortable by the minute. I had a feeling this was leading to something. "I suppose," I said. "What I mean is, I'm not ruling it out. But I can't say I'm really looking, either."

"But you'd know it if you saw, wouldn't you?"

Taking the opportunity to take a long drink of Coke, I tried to think quickly, but my powers of reasoning seemed have departed for regions unknown. I began noticing her perfume, although that could have been due to the fact that she seemed to be edging closer to me. If I was going to get out of there, now was the time. I stood up.

"I'd better let you get your sleep," I said. "You've had a long day."

If she was disappointed or offended, she didn't show it as she stood up also and walked me to the door. "See you tomorrow?"

The words were full of implication, but I merely nodded, said goodnight, and walked quickly to my car. I got behind the wheel and closed the door, fastening my seatbelt out of habit. I put the key in the ignition, but waited for a moment before turning the key. Instead, I just sat there, trying to sort through what had just happened.

First, Leslie sleeps with his date and offers her a job. Next thing I know, she's coming onto me in a major way. Was I happy about this? Strangely, I wasn't sure. I knew Leslie wouldn't be and that was a big reason why I shouldn't be. After all, I had just assured him that nothing was going on between me and Sarah. Of course, the argument could be made that at the time I said that, it had been true. At least, to my knowledge.

I started the car and pulled onto the street, making for the highway. Once on the onramp, I began accelerating to merge. Traffic wasn't bad, but I hated people who couldn't merge and if being a bit over-aggressive was necessary to avoid becoming like them, then so be it.

I reached down to turn on the radio, but paused as something caught my eye. What had it been? A shadow, a movement...maybe it had actually been a soft, subtle sound from behind. My eyes flicked up to the rearview mirror and I got quite a jolt as I saw someone sitting in the backseat.

"Holy crap!"

I grabbed for my Glock, but a strong hand grasped my right arm and pinned it to the seat.

"No need to be hasty," the man said.

"You, uh...kind of startled me, Nick. You're a creepy man in the daylight, but take on Transylvanic qualities when abruptly spotted sitting in the back seats of people's cars as the sun is setting."

"Sorry, didn't mean to frighten you," Nick Gantry said. "No, that isn't true. I *did* mean to frighten you. But I didn't figure it would matter much in the long run."

"How long of a run?"

"Not long. You see, Carter, you've really been on my case, lately. Ever since I got back into town, you've been trailing me, staking out my house, and making a general nuisance of yourself. Now you have the cops looking for me, too. All because some stupid brat didn't know enough to look both ways before crossing the street."

"That 'stupid brat' is hanging by a thread as we speak," I said, entertaining an intense desire to beat this idiot's brains out.

"Hey, a news flash," Gantry said. "The world's a tough place. Let me get right to the point, here. I'm a guy who doesn't like being annoyed. I'm annoyed. And I'm annoyed because of you. Therefore, you have to go. See, that's logic."

"Actually, that's murder," I corrected. "And I don't think it would help your cause any."

"But I'd be a lot happier. Without you, I could just leave the state and settle somewhere else. I could shake the cops, all right, but you'd be liable to follow me around and the whole process would just start all over again. That would really tick me off, see, so I figured I'd just finish it right here and be done with it."

"How ambitious of you," I said, stomping on the accelerator.

"What the hell are you doing?" Gantry was thrown off balance by the sudden burst of speed and I heard him scrambling around in the backseat.

"Not wearing your seatbelt, eh?" I said. "Tsk, tsk."

By the time I felt the cold barrel of Gantry's gun at the back of my head, I was doing seventy and still accelerating.

"Stop the car, Carter!"

"So you can kill me? I think not." The speedometer passed eighty. "You see, Gantry, if you kill me, the car goes out of control. Then we both die. Somehow, I don't think that's part of your plan."

I was pushing eighty-five and Gantry was screaming obscenities at me, telling me to stop the car and pull over. I grinned at him in the mirror and shook my head.

"Not until I run out of gas or blow the engine," I said. "And neither of those things is going to happen any time soon." The gun barrel was still pressed firmly against my head. "Better move that gun, Gantry. Like I said, if I die, you die and with all the potholes around here, it'd be a shame if…"

The gun moved slightly and in the mirror I saw the barrel clear the side of my head. With the knowledge that an inadvertent shot wouldn't hit me, I slammed on the brakes and braced myself against the steering wheel and the back of the seat.

Even though I was prepared for the sudden stop, I was thrown forward with incredible force. My seatbelt caught and held. Gantry was not so lucky.

Having irresponsibly ignored the constant warnings by the State Police to wear his safety belt, Nick Gantry was tossed over the front seat like a rag doll, nearly impaling himself on the gearshift. I heard the air rush from his lungs and he gagged mightily.

"Not in my car!"

We had come to a complete stop by now and I threw open the driver's door and dragged the other man out just as he began throwing up all over himself. My leather seats were saved.

Convinced Gantry wouldn't soon be going anywhere under his own power, I went back to the car and retrieved his weapon. Also retrieving my cell phone, I placed a quick call to Gary, who promised be on the scene shortly.

"Hear that, Nick?" I said, turning around to face my captive.

Apparently, Nick Gantry had no concept regarding the proper behavior of a captive, because he was ignoring one of the cardinal rules of captivity. One should stay where one is put. Nick Gantry was nowhere to be seen.

Chapter Fourteen

The ringing of the doorbell startled Jonny as he was just settling down into a tub full of steaming bath water. The resulting flinch caused his left foot to slip on the wet, slippery side of the tub and he plunged into the water, landing heavily on his rear with a muted thump.

"Damn!"

The doorbell rang again and Jonny struggled out of the tub and grabbed a towel. He slipped again on the wet tile floor, but caught himself on the sink and managed to regain his balance.

Who could be at the door? Whoever it was, it couldn't be good. It was eleven o'clock at night, so it couldn't be a package delivery. He hadn't ordered anything, besides. He had set up residence here for the express purpose of remaining incognito until Markoski was dead.

The ringing had lapsed into a measured knocking, which grew more and more insistent. Jonny wrapped the large towel around his middle and splashed across the bathroom floor.

Upon reaching the hallway, he paused for a moment to retrieve a small .38 revolver from a desk drawer before proceeding to the front door. He peered out the peephole and saw a short, heavy-set man dressed in a Papa John's pizza uniform, holding an insulated container.

"What the...? I didn't order any pizza."

Deciding the man must have the wrong address, Jonny pushed the revolver into the side of the towel and reached up to undo the chain and then the deadbolt.

The moment the bolt slid back, the door burst open. The man dropped the pizza box, revealing a scary sawed-off shotgun. The door hit Jonny squarely in the chest and he fell backward, struggling to catch his breath as the doorknob caught him in the abdomen. The revolver fell from the towel and he instinctively grabbed for it, but the intruder kicked it away and pumped the action on the shotgun, leveling it directly at Jonny's groin.

"Another move and Jonny, Jr.'ll be singing a rhythm and blues number," the man said, smiling happily at his own cleverness. "A real sad, sad song."

Jonny scooted backward across the floor, but the gun muzzle followed his every move.

"Who are you? What the hell is going on?"

"Perhaps I'm not the best person to answer that question," the man said. He stepped aside and a tall, older man with a cane limped through the door.

"Markoski!"

"In the flesh. Nice to see you, Jonathon." Markoski smiled at the sight of Jonny's attire. "Hope we didn't interrupt anything. May we come in?"

"Would it make a difference if I said no?"

Markoski shook his head. "No. Except that it might make me very angry."

"In that case," Jonny said, shrugging, "make yourselves at home. Could I interest you in a beverage?"

Markoski smiled in approval. "I admire your ability to remain calm under pressure, Jonathon. And, yes, I could use a beverage. Water with lemon would be quite refreshing."

"The kitchen's that way." Jonny pointed the way. "Have Charlie get it."

Charlie looked questioningly at Markoski, who nodded. "If you please, Charles. Water with lemon. You may leave me the handgun."

Charlie hesitated a moment before giving Markoski the .38 and disappearing in the direction of the kitchen.

"Glasses are in the cabinet just above the sink," Jonny shouted after him. "Don't break any. They're one of a kind."

Markoski laughed. "You always did have balls, Jonathon. Your backbone made you a valuable employee of mine. But it also made you dangerous. I think I knew all along that it would come to this eventually, but I never wanted to believe it."

"Come to what?" Jonny asked. "What is this all about? Have I done something?"

"You're a smooth one, Jonathon, but even your silver tongue isn't going to get you out of this. You know very well why I'm here. I believe you even expected it, at least in some way. Ah, thank you." Charles had returned with the lemon water. Markoski took a small sip and nodded his approval. "Nothing quite like the refreshing effect of citrus."

"I still don't follow you," Jonny insisted. "You seem to be operating under the false impression that I've done something against you. I can assure you —"

"Please..." Markoski raised one aged hand. "Don't compound your treason by lying. I know you've been plotting my demise ever since you came to see me in Chicago."

"I—"

"I know you've been enlisting the help of third parties to not only find me, but to carry out the actual deed. You're a complicated man, Jonathon. You are obviously a man of courage and resource, yet you hire out the jobs for which you would be best suited. Could it be that you still harbor some affection for the old days?"

"Certainly, I do," Jonny said. "I long for the old days, in fact. That is why these accusation are not only false, but ridiculous. Who's been filling your head with these lies?"

"A very reliable source," Markoski said.

"May I ask who?"

"You may ask," the older man said, "but I'm afraid I cannot reveal the source. Suffice it to say, they are in a position to know the information they have passed on to me."

"And you trust them over me?"

Markoski nodded. "It is a sad reality of the business that one must operate on the assumption that the worst-case scenario is the accurate one. I didn't want to believe the news, Jonathon, but when presented with the proof, there was no recourse."

"So you're going to kill me." It was a statement, not a question. Jonny had known ever since Markoski had appeared what was in store. The bluff was a last-ditch effort, a desperate attempt to appeal to the old man's desire to rekindle the glory of the old days, which would certainly not include having his closest confidants turn on him. It had been a long shot, at best.

"I'm afraid so, Jonathon. I needn't tell you how this saddens me," Markoski said, although his impassive voice betrayed no such emotion. "If there was some way to prevent this, be sure I would find it. However, those who turn against me have always been made to pay. I cannot change that now. You made your choice."

Markoski leaned heavily against the counter, while Johnny struggled to his feet under the watchful gaze of his own revolver, which was now pointed directly at his face.

"You're a very clever man," Markoski continued, *"which also gives me cause to regret the present circumstances. Fortunately, I am also clever. And I have a lifetime of experience behind me. Did you really think you would get away with plotting to murder me, Jonathon? Really, I find that highly insulting. Not so much the murder, but the fact you thought you could get away with it. Did you forget who you were dealing with or did you simply consider me past my prime? Too old to keep up with you? Senile, perhaps?"*

Jonny shook his head. *"None of the above, actually. But I decided before I was ever out of prison that I would never be a robot again."*

"A robot?"

"Yes, Markoski. A robot." Jonny's voice took on a hard edge and disregarding the weapon in the other man's hand, took a step forward. As he spoke, his voice rose slowly, until he was almost screaming. *"For years I obeyed your every command without question. I killed for you. I stole for you. I lied and sent men to their deaths for you. All because you were Markoski, the great Markoski, and because you were going to take care of us all. As long as we stuck with you, you said, we would never have any worries. I believed it! I swallowed the lie!"*

Jonny took a deep breath, swallowed, and regained control. His voice returned to normal and his reddened face relaxed. *"And then came the day when the world fell apart and I found myself standing in a courtroom, condemned, while you escaped. Thwarted the system. I and all the others paid for your crimes, Markoski. That's why I did what I did, even though I knew I would likely be discovered. It was worth the risk. It was worth it for the chance to see you die, Markoski! Worth it to know you felt the same agonies you gave to others."*

During much of the speech, Markoski had remained impassive. Slowly, however, as Jonny continued to speak, the man's mouth tightened and his eyes squinted. A vein popped out on his neck and a bead of sweat trickled down his forehead.

"It is gratifying to hear you speak so frankly, Jonathon," he said, his finger tightening on the trigger. His hand shook ever so slightly as the rage inside built. "So many times a leader must wonder if what his underlings are saying is true or if they are merely paying him service. Now that I know how you truly feel, I needn't bother feeling gloomy about this."

Markoski pulled the trigger on the .38 and a slug ripped into Jonny's left knee. Blood began streaming down the leg and Jonny collapsed onto the floor as if hit in the head with a brick. His mouth opened in a scream, but horribly, no sound came out.

"Was it really worth it, Jonathon?" Markoski asked. He smiled and fired another shot, this one finding its mark in Jonny's right knee.

This time, the scream was real. The sound and misery of it filled the small room. Jonny flopped onto his side like a fish, trying to grasp his shattered knees simultaneously to stop both the bleeding and the pain. Both attempts failed. He screamed again.

"Now that's much too loud," Markoski said, raising the gun for another shot. "We might wake the neighbors." The third bullet entered Jonny's throat, instantly turning the screams into ghastly, gurgling sounds.

Markoski turned toward the door and beckoned for Charlie to follow. Halfway out the door, he stopped to glance back at the gruesome sight. Although not a man given to levity, Markoski laughed.

Chapter Fifteen

I got up the next morning and fixed myself some breakfast. I ate it slowly, my thoughts far away from fried eggs and bacon. I couldn't stop thinking about Sarah and the events of last night. I couldn't deny that there was a connection between us. Was my loyalty to Leslie ruining the possibility of a good relationship?

Of course, as Sarah had pointed out earlier, I was still wearing my wedding ring. That wasn't exactly a magnet for women. At least, not the kind of women with whom I'd want to enter into a relationship. The ring very plainly said that I was unavailable.

I wasn't sure why I was still wearing the ring. Maybe it was a defense mechanism, designed to protect me from having to deal with women. Or maybe I hadn't moved as far past Brooke as I liked to think. I certainly wasn't still in love with the woman, but having been so emotionally close to someone for years created a bond, no matter how the relationship ended. Perhaps I hadn't gotten over that. Suddenly disgusted at my own weakness, I pulled off the ring and tossed it over my shoulder in one fluid movement.

There. I was done with it. If I was smart, I'd retrieve it from where it had fallen under the window and take it down to the nearest pawn shop. It was a decent ring and a shame to waste, but the symbolism of tossing it aside like a rotting piece of garbage was too satisfying. I'd take care of it later.

After running a few errands, I arrived back at the office to find Sarah again working diligently at the filing. She had made an incredible dent in the stack. Working at this pace, she'd have the entire mess sorted out and filed within another day or two.

"An amazing job," I said, indicating the neatly arranged piles of paper and folders. "I really must give Leslie more credit for his hiring abilities."

Sarah smiled brightly and stood up from where she had been kneeling on the floor, sorting out papers. There were so many files that the floor was the only place big enough to work.

Her hair had become mussed and she brushed a few errant strands away from her face. "It's really fun work," she said. "I've enjoyed it."

I made a face in disgust. "Personally, I can't stand filing. I'd rather slide down a fifty-foot razor into a vat of acid than file papers. Hopefully, you'll be able to stay on here for awhile to keep things in order. Otherwise, in a few months, it'll be right back to the way it was."

"I wasn't planning to go anywhere." The sideways smile she gave me didn't seem particularly business-like. I also noticed her perfume for the first time. Not strong, barely noticeable, but present at the most unexpected moments.

She picked up a three-ring hole puncher and moved to place it back on my desk. The trip brought her right next to me and she didn't move away.

"What a day," she said. "Filing's fun, but exhausting work. Have you heard any more on the little boy? What was his name?"

"Derrick. No, I haven't heard anything. I'm assuming he's holding steady, at least. I need to call back up there and check on him."

"Leslie says you feel responsible for the accident."

"Leslie talks too much."

Sarah edged closer to me and I felt her right arm slide behind me. "It's not your fault, Kirk." Her voice was incredibly soft and the room became very warm. "You couldn't have changed anything."

I wasn't so sure about that, but at the moment, I was having trouble completing an intelligent thought. I wondered what Leslie would say if he were to walk in right about now. Perhaps his suspicions were not so unfounded after all.

"That's what I keep telling myself," I said, "but I'm afraid I'm not very convincing."

She laid her head against my shoulder and used her right arm to pull me closer. "Maybe you just need to get your mind off it for awhile," she said. "We've both had a busy couple of days."

I didn't know exactly what she meant by the suggestion, but I wasn't sure I liked the sound of it. I mean, I did, but...I didn't. It was time for an escape.

"Listen, Sarah, I need to make few phone calls, so..."

"Now?" Her laugh was soft and low. "You need to learn how to relax. Why are you so nervous? Didn't you feel that there was something between us last night? And yesterday morning?"

"Regardless of what I feel, Leslie still thinks of you as his," I said. "I'd just feel a lot better about all this if you'd talk to him."

"I don't think Leslie wants to hear what I have to say."

She had a point there. Leslie could be very stubborn and even if she did attempt to bring up the subject, he'd be likely to block it out. Especially if it started going in a direction contrary to his own template.

"I still think you should at least try to discuss it. If he chooses not to listen, then it's his problem. You've done your part."

Sarah reached up and tucked a few errant strands of hair behind my left ear. "But that would be so devastating to him," she argued. "Why destroy his fantasy world? He'll find another girl before long and then it won't matter."

"It just doesn't seem fair," I said. "If it were me, I'd want Leslie to at least let me know he was planning to cut in on me."

"So you do admit there's something between us?" Sarah wrapped her other arm around me, holding me tightly and looking up with a wide smile.

I nodded, relieved to have admitted it. Before I knew what was happening, she had started kissing me. *I should stop this,* I thought. *Suppose Leslie walked in again? After all my talk and assurances to him, he'd never be able to trust me again.*

I didn't stop, though. The kisses lengthened and deepened. Somehow, my sport coat ended up on the floor and Sarah was making admirable headway on my shirt when there was a buzzing sound as the front door of the office opened.

Both Sarah and I jumped as if we'd been tasered. She moved away from me and grabbed a handful of files in a vain attempt to appear busy. Her lipstick was impossibly smeared and I pointed mutely. She took my meaning and leaped for the bathroom to do some repair work.

I just stood there, still a little stunned, trying to take in what had just happened. I probably had lipstick on my face, but there was no mirror handy. If it was Leslie, then it was over. There was no way I was talking my way out of this one. I fumbled with the buttons on my shirt.

"Hello? What kind of lousy service is this?"

I wilted in relief as I recognized the voice. Walking into the main office, I saw Jackson Wyatt standing at the front desk. We exchanged bear hugs and then I stepped back.

"What are you doing in town? Did Chicago get too windy for you?"

"Actually, I have some information for you and decided to drive up and deliver. I was getting antsy and wanted to get out of town, anyway."

"Well, I hope you didn't come here to relax," I said. "It's been pretty lively."

"So I see." Jackson peered at me and grinned. "What happened, did you try to put on your makeup in the dark?"

I felt a red flush begin creeping up my neck. "It's nothing. Just a little misunderstanding. It's not what it looks like."

I heard the bathroom door open and Sarah came around the corner all business, makeup and hair perfectly in place and her arms full of files. She was a cool customer. In an attempt to rescue the situation, I turned to her.

"Sarah, this is Jackson Wyatt. Jackson, my secretary, Sarah."

"Hi," Jackson said, the smarmy grin still infesting his face. "Are you keeping this guy straight? If anyone can do it, you should be able to." He turned back to me. "Your hiring practices have improved since the last time I was here."

"Still the same Jackson," I said. "Still a chauvinist pig."

"I prefer chauvinist swine, actually," Jackson corrected. "It has a certain elegance, don't you think?"

"For you, yes. Have you eaten, swine?"

"Not since an hour ago," he said. "I'm starved."

"Well, then let's go grab something. You want to come, Sarah?"

She smiled gracefully and shook her head. "No, I'm making some real progress on this filing and don't want to lose my momentum. You two go ahead."

"Are you sure?" Jackson seemed eager for her to come along. "You look hungry."

Yeah, but not for food, I thought. *And since when are you worried about losing your momentum?*

"No, thanks," Sarah said. "I brought a lunch with me. I'll be fine."

"Okay, but you'll be missing out," Jackson said. "I've been told I'm fabulous company."

"He talks to himself," I explained. "It's a bad habit I've tried hard to get him to break, but he's stubborn. Or maybe just weak-willed."

"I have great willpower," Jackson protested. "I'm looking you in the face and still have an appetite. Now that's the measure of a man."

"Point taken. Let's go."

We arrived at Brann's Steakhouse and Grille just as they opened and once we were seated, Jackson perused the menu for few moments with a caustic eye.

"What's good here?"

"Everything," I said. The waitress, who had just arrived with our drinks, nodded in affirmation. "Personally, I would recommend either the 8 oz. steak or the half-pound burger. They'll both make you want to slap your grandmother."

"That good, huh? I think I'll try the burger."

"And I'll have the steak."

The waitress smiled brightly. "Both excellent choices. That'll be about ten minutes." She took our menus and disappeared into the kitchen. Jackson watched her go.

"I'm starting to be glad I let you talk me into this. The only part I don't care for is some of the décor. Why do they have a mannequin falling out of the ceiling?"

"You got me there," I said. "Does it really matter?"

"I just keep feeling like I should jump up and help the poor guy. That looks incredibly painful."

"Forget about it. Once the food arrives, you'll forget all about him."

My promise proved true a few minutes later, when Jackson took his first bite of the famous, local burger.

"Sweet mercy. That's rather tasty."

"Still feel sorry for the guy in the ceiling?"

Jackson shook his head and said cruelly, "Let him get his own burger." He took another large bite, chewed twice, and swallowed.

"So what's this hot information you have for me?" I asked. "It must be pretty important, considering you got out of bed just to deliver it to me."

For once, Jackson ignored the jibe. "I thought it was important," he said seriously. "That's one reason I actually drove up here to break it to you."

"Too hot for the phone line?" Now he had me curious.

"I didn't want to say this at the office, because I wasn't sure what kind of security clearance Miss Splendor had," Jackson said, "but the Markoski situation might be more serious than previously thought."

"How so?"

"Well, you know he wanted you dead to begin with."

I nodded. "Right. I'm the one who told you that."

"Have you heard about Louie's murder?"

"News travels fast," I said, nodding once again. "I found the body. So far, none of this is news, Jackson. Tell me you have more."

"Do you know Jonny Bushetti?"

The name gave me reason for pause. "I can't say that I *know* him. I spoke to him yesterday."

"Talking to you must be bad luck," Jackson observed. "That somewhat confirms my suspicions."

I felt a chill run up my neck. "Why?" I thought I already knew the answer.

"He's dead. Shot to death."

"Markoski?"

"As far as I've been able to find out. Nobody knows much or is simply not talking. I wouldn't blame them. At this rate, anyone who opens their mouth will be dead within twenty-four hours."

"I'll say. Markoski works fast."

"He always has been a speedy worker," Jackson said, "but this has to be a record even for him."

"How is he discovering all this stuff? He must have spies everywhere."

"That's the real reason I drove up here," Jackson said. "I started wondering the same thing. How does Markoski know all these things? Obviously, the guy isn't omnipresent, so there has to be a connection somewhere. I could only come up with one."

"And that would be?"

"You."

I was shocked. "Me?"

"Not you personally, but yes. Think about it. Louie meets with you and dies two days later. Jonny Buschetti contacts you and dies the next day. Both of these individuals are notoriously close-mouthed, so I can't imagine them spreading the word regarding their intentions. So the question remains. How did Markoski know?"

"You think I have a spy?"

"Not necessarily. But I wouldn't be surprised if someone on your staff is unwisely talking to someone outside the operation. It wouldn't take much. Markoski may not be the powerhouse crime boss he once was, but he still has a network to be envied."

I thought for a moment. "Leslie can get a little talkative," I said. "If he ever decides to show up for work, I'll have a talk with him and see who he's been hanging around."

"Are these his normal working hours?" Jackson asked. "Or does he have any normal working hours?"

"He's always been a little cavalier about his schedule," I said, "but he's generally in before eleven o' clock. If not, then there's a reason and he calls me. I'll call him after we're done eating and see what the story is. Hopefully, it'll be a good one."

Chapter Sixteen

As it turned out, I didn't call Leslie right away. It was still relatively early, just after noon, and I was sure Leslie would be at the office when we returned. Not being particularly worried, I spent another couple of hours showing Jackson around the city.

Once the grand tour was completed, I called the office and was informed by Sarah that Leslie had still not made a personal appearance or even called to explain his absence.

I put in calls to both Leslie's cell phone and home phone. Both went unanswered. I closed my phone and slipped it into my pocket.

"I'm not sure if I should be worried or angry," I said. "Leslie can be exceptionally irresponsible at times, but this a little over the top, even for him. Worse, tonight is when we're supposed to escort Mrs. Chandler to the shin-dig at DeVos Place. I need Leslie there to watch my back."

"Do you expect trouble?"

"Not really, but you have to plan for the worst. Maybe we should drive by and check his house."

Jackson nodded in agreement and we drove to East Grand Rapids, where Leslie maintained an impressive residence. Jackson whistled at the sight.

"You two must be doing well in your little venture."

"We're doing all right, but Leslie has dear old dad to thank for most of this. He's been sponsoring us for a few years. Now we're independent enough that it's completely unnecessary, but Leslie insists that it would hurt his father if we decided we didn't need him, so I haven't said anything."

"And you like the extra money."

I shrugged. "Honestly, I'd just as soon get along without it. At the beginning, it was a blessing, but now it makes me feel reliant. I hate that. But, unfortunately, I can't think of a way to extricate myself from the situation without appearing ungrateful, which I'm certainly not."

I put the car into park and got out. Jackson followed close behind as I walked up to the front door and began banging unceremoniously. After an unfruitful minute of this, I finally gave up and took to skulking around the outside of the house, peering in windows and then trying the latches.

"You're going to get us arrested," Jackson said, still following. "This is obviously an upscale area and we have to look highly suspicious."

"Something just doesn't seem right," I mused, pushing on a bedroom window. It was locked. "The more I think about this, the more worried I am. It's after two o' clock. Leslie would have at least called by now. He knows we have a security detail in a few hours. He loves those assignments."

"Try calling him again."

Although I wasn't optimistic, I saw few options, so I pulled out my cell and dialed Leslie's home number. From where we stood, Jackson and I could hear the ringing from inside the house. It rang several times and the machine picked up. I cancelled the call.

"Well, we're definitely at the right house," Jackson said. "And he's definitely not here. Try his cell."

I was already punching in the numbers. We waited while the connection was made and then looked at each other in surprise and alarm. We could also hear that phone ringing.

"Something's wrong, here," I said. "Leslie takes his cell phone everywhere."

"Is he a heavy sleeper?"

"Not that I know of. Besides, he never sleeps this late." I took a quick glance around and, seeing no one, took my Glock from its holster.

"You can't shoot your way in there," Jackson protested. "The whole neighborhood would hear it."

"I'm not going to shoot," I said, and to demonstrate the truth of my words, I grasped the weapon by the barrel and used the butt to break the window. "Give me a boost."

Jackson did so and, being careful to avoid the scattered shards of glass, I slid through the opening and fell to the floor just below the window. I had kept my weapon out, just in case, and now crouched in the shadows and surveyed the room.

The curtains were drawn over most of the windows, making the interior of the house quite dark. Seeing any potential threats was nearly impossible, since my eyes had not yet fully adjusted, so I remained where I was until I was able to make out details.

"Kirk." It was Jackson, whispering from outside the house.

"I don't see anything," I whispered back. "Can you get through the window?"

"If you give me a hand up."

I did so and, within a few seconds, Jackson was crouched next to me.

"The cell phone has to be close," I said. "The ringers on those things aren't that loud and I could hear it pretty clear from outside." I began moving around the room slowly, checking every nook and cranny.

Jackson also began looking and startled me with a sudden exclamation. "I think I found it! It was on the floor and I just kicked it under the coffee table." He bent and plucked out the phone, but dropped it just as quickly with an expletive.

"What's the matter?"

"It's wet," he said, looking at his hand. "I can't tell for sure in this light, but I think it's blood."

The word sent a shock through me and I abandoned all pretense of stealth. "Leslie!"

I began walking through the house, turning on every light I came to and shouting Leslie's name. Finally, as I passed the bathroom, I heard a slight movement and a gasp. I jerked open the door.

"Kirk—"

"Leslie! What the...oh, *shit!*"

My partner lay slumped against the side of the bathtub, both himself and the tile floor covered in blood. I started inside, slipped on the wet tiles, and had to catch myself by grabbing the towel rack. After regaining my balance, I bent down close to Leslie. His face was chalky and beaded with sweat. He managed a shaky grin, but his voice was weak.

"It would appear that I'm rather late for work."

"Yeah." I tried to smile back. "You're fired. Jackson! In the bathroom!" I turned back to Leslie. "What happened?"

"Gantry."

"Nick Gantry?"

Leslie nodded and the movement seemed to exhaust him. "He sneaked into the house and hit me. I was only semi-conscious, but I faintly remember being dragged in here and propped against the tub. I could hear them talking."

"What did they do to you?"

Leslie motioned faintly downward with his chin. I looked and saw two ragged gashes, one on each wrist.

"They were trying to make it look like suicide," he said. "By the time I came around enough to really understand what was going on, I had lost too much blood. Too weak. I've only been awake a couple of minutes."

Jackson appeared in the doorway and I tossed him my cell. He knew what to do.

"You said 'they,' Leslie. Who was here besides Gantry?"

"Don't...know. I didn't recognize him. They were working for Markoski, though."

"They said that?"

Leslie nodded. "They wanted me out of the way for tonight."

"Tonight? The security detail?"

"Somehow, they knew we were going to be guarding the Chandlers tonight and wanted to get us out of the way. I think they're planning to kill Mr. Chandler."

"Why would they—"

"He used to be a prosecutor," Leslie said. He was slipping fast and his words were coming in snatches. "Was involved in the...Markoski case."

I thought back and suddenly remembered. Leslie was right. Chandler had been in charge of the Markoski prosecution. He had been the one to make the legal error that resulted in the crime boss's release. In other words, he would be on Markoski's personal hit list. That explained the anonymous threats Mrs. Chandler had mentioned.

No wonder it all seemed so random. Markoski was hiring out his killings and all his hitmen kept turning on him and, consequently, dying. Nick Gantry must be the latest. Convenient, too, since he was already in town.

Unless, of course, he had been involved all along and that was why he was here to begin with. That would make even more sense, considering he'd been available to kill Louie. That would also explain why he was so desperate to escape a couple of days ago when he realized I was tailing him. He had no way of knowing how much I knew. It was all falling into place.

"The ambulance is on its way," Jackson said, handing me back my cell phone. "How's he doing?"

Leslie looked up at him and tried to smile, but managed only to move his lips a bit. "Well enough to...whip your sorry bum," he said. He turned back to me. "Promise me you'll get this bastard."

I nodded, listening desperately for the sound of an approaching ambulance, willing it to arrive on time. "I promise. But first, we're going to make sure you're okay."

After what seemed like hours, paramedics rushed into the house, shown in by Jackson, who had waited by the front door. I had made a crude attempt to stop the bleeding in the meantime, but Leslie had lost so much blood prior to my arrival that my efforts seemed to do little good.

For the next couple of hours, Jackson and I sat in the emergency waiting room, not speaking, but plotting the demise of both Nick Gantry and Roderick Markoski.

Finally, the doctor came out and, with a simple shake of his head, told us what we had been expecting to hear. Leslie was gone.

Chapter Seventeen

The evening dragged by. I hadn't wanted to come to the party at all, given the circumstances, but I had made a promise to Leslie and, if Gantry was intending to kill Mr. Chandler tonight, then following through on my commitment to serve as security for the family was the best way to keep an eye out for him.

I had enlisted Jackson's help. Fortunately, I kept an extra pistol in the glove box, a .38 revolver he could slip into his jacket pocket. Because we hadn't had time to go back to the office before meeting the Chandlers at their house, we had come straight from the hospital and must have looked terrible.

"I must say," Mrs. Chandler had said, "you certainly don't look as if you're planning to attend a black-tie affair. I thought I specifically asked you to be inconspicuous."

At her insistence, Jackson and I had been outfitted with formal wear. Being leftovers from her two sons' wardrobes, the suits were somewhat ill-fitting, but we bore the indignity with grace. To attend the party wearing our wrinkled casuals would certainly not assist in our attempt to remain discreet. At least now we should be able to blend in reasonably well as long as neither of us tried to bend over or sit down.

While at the hospital, I had tried to call Sarah, but received no answer. I tried again en route to the Chandlers, but again received no answer. Assuming she had simply left for the day, I had put the matter out of my mind and concentrated on the task ahead.

So far, we had seen no sign of Nick Gantry. The event had been going well and I was pleased to discover that a portion of the proceeds would be going into a fund to help Derrick's family with the medical bills. I donated all I had on me, wishing I had known about the charity so I could have brought my check book.

Jackson tapped me on the shoulder. "Any sign?"

"Not yet," I said. "We don't even know if he'll try anything here. He might wait until they get home. And don't forget that we're looking for more people than just Gantry. Leslie mentioned another man he didn't recognize."

"We'll just have to keep our eyes on Chandler at all times," Jackson said. "That shouldn't be too difficult." He pointed toward the platform, where Mr. Chandler was holding up his hand and trying to get everyone's attention.

"I trust everyone is having a good time," he said, once he had managed to quiet the room. The crowd applauded in response. "As one of the sponsors of tonight's event, I just wanted to thank everyone for coming and remind you all of the worthy charity we are presenting. It was a last minute thing and we apologize for springing it on everyone, but it only happened a couple of days ago."

As Mr. Chandler continued speaking, Jackson nudged me. "Why do I get the feeling that this is more about Mr. Chandler than the kid?"

"Because you're a wise man."

Mr. Chandler prattled on for several more minutes, before finally responding to a signal from his wife to shut up.

"Now, before we all continue with this fine evening, I propose a toast." He looked down and realized his glass was empty. He grinned sheepishly. "But first I'll have to refresh my drink. The night's still young, you know."

The crowd laughed politely and I watched as one of the waiters scrambled to give Mr. Chandler a wine glass.

"To the evening," Mr. Chandler said, raising his glass. "May there be many more like it." He put the glass to his lips and drank.

It seemed as if I was watching from afar, like a movie being played out before me. Mr. Chandler drank, swallowed, and then staggered. Jackson and I looked at each other and then ran for the platform.

By the time we got through the crowd, Mr. Chandler had already collapsed. He was retching and starting to go into convulsions. A man pushed his way up to us. He identified himself as a doctor and began working on the victim.

I looked around just in time to see the waiter who had given Mr. Chandler the glass, slipping out a side door.

Grabbing Jackson's arm, I started running back into the crowd. It was slow going, as most of the people were clustering around the victim, craning their necks to see what had happened. Jackson and I pushed our way through without reservation. Men in tuxedos and women in fine dresses went sprawling as we barged through.

Even so, by the time we exited the side door and found ourselves outside, the fake waiter was already across Monroe Street and running into the parking ramp.

"It must have been the other man Leslie mentioned," I said, running across the street without looking both ways. "Gantry would know I'd recognize him. Naturally, he wouldn't come."

We stopped running when we reached the ramp entrance and proceeded with more caution. Our quarry was doubtless armed and would have no compunction about taking us out if he saw the opportunity.

We split up and walked slowly through the parked cars, guns at the ready, searching every shadow and backseat we came to. After several minutes, we met up again and Jackson held up his hands in a gesture of ignorance.

"No sign of him," he said. "You think he made it to another floor?"

"Maybe. I think we would've—"

My words were interrupted by the roar of a car engine. We were flooded with light as a pair of headlights flicked on and the squeal of tires filled the close confines of the parking ramp.

I barely had time to turn around before the car was speeding toward us. I was already holding my Glock, so I raised it and took a precious couple of seconds to aim at the shadowy form behind the steering wheel. The car passed under a light and I recognized Gantry behind the wheel, while the phony waiter sat in the passenger seat.

Time to die, you dirty son of a bitch.

Jackson jumped for it, but I was too mad and perhaps not thinking clearly. Regardless, I had just enough time to see the sneering expression on Gantry's face before I began pulling the trigger.

Several holes appeared in the windshield and the car swerved as one of the rounds found its target. Completely out of control, the vehicle sideswiped several parked cars before crashing directly into the concrete barrier.

After the initial cacophony of the impact, it seemed oddly quiet, the only sound being the engine of the car, which had somehow kept operating. Gradually, I became aware of something that sounded like running water. Jackson sniffed.

"Is that what I think it is?"

"What do you think it is?"

"Gas."

I sniffed as well and noticed a pool of liquid covering the concrete floor underneath the crashed vehicle.

"Perhaps we should...."

"Run?"

"Yeah."

We didn't get but a few feet before the heat from the exhaust pipe ignited the gasoline and the entire vehicle exploded in flames. The force of the blast threw both of us to the floor and the wind was knocked from my lungs. I lay on the hard concrete for a full minute, struggling to breathe and figure out what happened. To my left, Jackson groaned and rolled over onto his back.

"What the hell was that?"

"Either a house landed on us or you've once again ignored my friendly warnings to avoid Mexican food."

"All that from a gas leak? Seems a little extreme. That explosion just about tore me in two."

"Maybe they were burning premium."

A glare from Jackson told me that he didn't appreciate my humor, so I simply pushed myself up and stood teetering. The force of the explosion seemed to have screwed around with my inner ear. I looked at the burning wreck and couldn't help feeling a small amount of triumph. I felt that Leslie had been avenged. And it had been stylish. He would have liked that.

I put the car into gear, backed out of the parking space, and pulled onto the street. The party had come to a sudden halt following the death of Mr. Chandler, but Jackson and I had spent hours telling and retelling our stories to the police.

"It's late," I said to Jackson. "You can crash at my place for now and we'll pick up tomorrow morning."

Both of us were worn out and on the verge of passing out from sheer exhaustion. I struggled to keep my eyes open as I drove toward my downtown condo and was too busy keeping the Eclipse on the road to notice a black SUV pull in behind us. It kept pace and when I parked along the curb, it pulled into an empty space a few lengths back.

"I've been thinking," Jackson said.

"I appreciate the warning," I said, laughing despite my exhaustion or, perhaps, because of it. "What brought that on?"

"My brilliant, analytical mind," he retorted. "The more I think about it, the more I wonder how all these pieces fit together. How does Markoski know every move we make?"

"You mean about tonight?"

"Not just tonight. How about Louie and Jonny? Who told on them?"

I thought about it for a moment. "As I said, Leslie could be quite talkative and he wasn't always judicious about his audience. Especially if there was a...pretty girl involved." My words dropped off as a terrible thought entered my mind. Jackson noticed the pause and the widening of my eyes.

"Sarah?"

I nodded. "She knew about Louie. And she was in the office with me when I took the call from Jonny Buschetti. She also knew about the Chandlers. From what she said, she even knew Mrs. Chandler personally, even worked for her at one time."

"How much do you actually know about her?"

"Not much. Nothing, really. Leslie brought her in and we both know Leslie's taste in women. I thought maybe he had finally found a winner."

"We don't know she's the leak," Jackson cautioned, holding up one hand. "Let's not jump to conclusions."

"The evidence strongly suggests it, though. As far we know, however, she has no reason to think we suspect anything. We'll confront her tomorrow at the office."

We pulled ourselves out of the car and walked slowly up the sidewalk to the front of the building. A couple flights of stairs later and we were standing in front of my door.

"I'm assuming you have a guest room, right?" Jackson asked, as I worked the key in the lock. "I don't do well with floors or air mattresses."

"No, but I have a semi-comfortable couch that's more than you deserve," I said. The stiff lock finally yielded and we walked inside. I flipped a switch and light abounded. Jackson took an appreciative look around.

"Not bad," he said. "You obviously called in an interior designer."

"How'd you know?"

"For starters, the color scheme is actually tasteful. And you're not using a crate as a table."

I laughed. "That was in college and I haven't done that since. Give me a break, it was all I could afford."

Jackson walked to the window and pulled back the shade. "Hey, not a bad view from up here, either. Did they charge you extra?"

"No, they had pretty much already maxed the price out," I said. "You want a drink?"

Jackson turned to answer, but just then his right foot slipped on something and he landed on the floor with a thump. At the same instant, the window in front of which he had just been standing, shattered.

"Holy crap!" Jackson wisely stayed down as he examined his person for any damage. He found none until he felt a warm trickle down his neck and discovered he was missing an earlobe.

I crept back to the door, made sure it was locked, and killed the lights. "How the hell did that bullet miss you?"

"I slipped on something," Jackson answered. We were both whispering for some reason. It just seemed appropriate. He felt around for a moment before finding the life-saving item. "It feels like a ring," he said.

My wedding ring. It had remained where I had thrown it, waiting patiently to save Jackson's life.

"Are they gone?"

Jackson slowly peered over the window sill, his left hand pressed tightly against his ear to staunch the flow of blood. "Considering I don't know where the shot came from, it's impossible to tell for sure. Everything seems quiet, though. I see brake lights down the street a ways. Maybe that's them making a getaway."

"Could be." I got to my feet and replaced the blind before turning the lights back on. "I doubt they'd stick around to examine their work. Better to get out before the cops arrive. Even if they think they got you, they know there's two of us. They must have followed us back here."

"I'm beginning to think these guys mean business," Jackson said facetiously. "Even considering the miss, that was a damn fine shot. If they did indeed shoot from a vehicle in the street, it was a weird, upward angle. Plus the deflection of the glass and my sudden movement..." He shuddered. "Maybe I'll take that drink, now."

Chapter Eighteen

The black Cadillac eased out of the Gerald R. Ford International Airport onto Patterson Avenue. Markoski's flight had just landed in Grand Rapids and he was eager to be in direct control of the situation. Everything had been going wrong and he was anxious to stop the bleeding. Carter was the final target left and one near and dear to Markoski's heart. He hadn't come this far to be stymied now.

Already, he was a day behind schedule. He had wanted all the jobs completed by the anniversary of his defeat, but that was not to be. Ah, well, it was but a small thing. Perhaps it was better this way, as long as Carter met death today. Now Markoski would get to mete out justice himself.

Markoski held the cell phone to his ear and listened carefully, a deep scowl etching his face into a valley of displeasure. How so many fools could have been in his organization was amazing to him. First, both Louie and Jonathon had turned on him and now it appeared that the men who had attempted to carry out his orders may have failed. He was still waiting confirmation on the success or failure of that mission, but from the initial report, it seemed that the shooter had missed his target.

After several more minutes of waiting, the line clicked and a voice came on the line.

"Sir?"

"Still waiting."

There was a pause and the sheer implication of the silence caused Markoski's blood pressure to rise to dangerous levels.

"Jackson is still alive."

"How do you know?"

"We just spotted both men leaving the condominium together."

Markoski exploded. "Imbecile bastard! What kind of fools are you! Where are they headed?"

"They haven't yet reached their vehicle, sir."

"They're probably going to the office. I'm on my way, but need a bit more time. Slow them down. Don't make it obvious, but don't let them leave right away. If possible, go ahead and finish the job of killing Jackson. We don't need him getting in the way. But leave Carter for me. Kill him and I'll have your hands cut off."

Markoski hung up and cursed again, hoping that this time his orders would be followed implicitly.

After hanging up with Markoski, the man nodded to his partner and got out of the vehicle. They began walking across Broadway Street, just as Carter and Jackson exited the building.

"Excuse me!" The first man quickened his pace and jogged toward them, taking out his wallet and flashing a fake ID as he approached. *"My name's Johnson. I'm with the Grand Rapids Police Department. We got a report of some strange happenings here last night. Did either of you see or hear anything?"*

"You're just now showing up to investigate?" Jackson asked, looking first at the speaker and then at the man's partner, who was just now approaching. *"It must not have been too serious."*

The man shrugged. *"We weren't sure what to make of it. The report was quite vague and we've gotten false reports from this building before, so we didn't feel it was a high priority."*

"What sort of strange happenings?" Kirk asked.

Again, the man shrugged. *"You tell me. Like I said, the report was vague. Neither of you saw or heard anything strange?"*

Jackson and Kirk looked at each other and shook their heads. *"Nope,"* Jackson said. *"Can't say that we did. But if we hear anything, like maybe gunshots, we'll let you know."*

"By the way," Kirk said, *"I didn't get a good look at that ID the first time. Could I have another peek at it?"*

"Not necessary," the man said. *"We're just asking a few preliminary questions."*

"Right," Kirk said, *"but I'm a concerned member of the public who just wants to make sure he's talking to a real police officer. That's why you guys carry badges and ID in the first place, isn't it? To identity yourselves to the public?"*

The man was getting the distinct impression that both Carter and Jackson were merely toying with him. It angered him and he wanted to pull out his .45 and let them both have it, but he knew Markoski would be furious. Besides, Carter's hand was staying suspiciously close to the inside of his sport coat.

"My ear hurts," Jackson said randomly. *"I need some Tylenol. Either of you two fellas have any?"*

Both men shook their heads. They exchanged a glance. The encounter wasn't going well. They weren't sure how long Markoski wanted the other two men delayed, but it was probably longer than thirty seconds.

"How about we step back inside while my partner and I ask you a few more questions," said the first man, who had identified himself as Johnson. "As unlikely as it may seem, this could be a serious matter."

"We just told you we didn't see or hear anything suspicious," Kirk said. "My friend and I are quite busy at the moment. Why don't you two come back later today or perhaps follow us to my office. Being a member of the GRPD, you surely know where the Carter Detective Agency is?"

"Why, yes. Of course."

"We're headed there now," Kirk said, walking toward his car. "You're welcome to ask us all the questions you wish there."

"I'm afraid we can't do that, Mr. Carter," Johnson said, quickly pulling the .45 from its shoulder holster. "You see, that would make our boss very angry."

Carter's hand ducked into his coat, but Johnson shook his head and tightened his trigger finger. Carter relaxed and slowly let his hand fall to his side.

"And who's your boss?" he asked. "Markoski, I'm guessing? What does he have against my office? Hey, if he objects to the color scheme, I'm all over it. I'll call the painters today. That leather couch? It's history! I'm thinking he'd probably like something more modern. Maybe a lot of black. And stainless steel."

"I find your humor quite tiresome, Mr. Carter," Johnson said. "Please do not make me use excessive force."

Kirk laughed "Why not? Isn't killing me kind of the idea? Let's get this show on the road, then." He continued smiling and walked a few steps nearer to Johnson, who backed up to maintain the distance. "If my brand of humor annoys you, what would I have to do to make you fighting mad, Johnson, huh? Tell you a few knock-knock jokes? Make fun of your mother, perhaps?"

Johnson's eyes were locked on Kirk's and, for a moment, his partner glanced away from Jackson. Within the space of a second, Jackson had covered the ground between them and plowed into the man, knocking him off balance and directly between Carter and the .45.

Even as Jackson moved, Carter went for his own weapon and Johnson instinctively fired just as his partner, pushed by Jackson, stumbled backward into the line of fire. The bullet entered his right side, careened off a rib, and split the aorta. The dead man dropped the ground.

Kirk had his own weapon out by now and sent one well-placed shot between Johnson's eyes. The man dropped like a rock, the .45 falling from his hand and skittering on the pavement. Kirk stooped and picked it up.

"Here," he said, handing it to Jackson. "You may need this. It'll shoot the crap out of that little .38."

Chapter Nineteen

I parked the Eclipse in the Bridgewater Place parking ramp and we got out of the car. We checked our weapons one last time. Jackson put the revolver back into the glove compartment, having taken quite a shine to the bulkier .45.

"You think there'll be trouble in there?" Jackson asked.

I nodded. "Almost certainly. I didn't get the feeling that Johnson and his partner were there to simply kill us. They could have done that from their car. It was almost like they were just trying to slow us down. Delay us for some reason."

We walked to the building entrance and made our way to the office with no trouble or unusual occurrences. Everything seemed absurdly normal. The usual people were scurrying around. I gave and received the usual hellos. Everything was standard. And that was really creeping me out.

The door to the office was also normal. No signs of forced entry, although Sarah would still have her key. Markoski, if necessary, would have access to professionals.

I opened the door and stepped inside cautiously, although any element of surprise I may have hoped to obtain was summarily ruined by the door buzzer.

"I really should have that thing removed," I said. "I never liked it and it's very unprofessional."

Jackson opened his mouth as if to reply, but before he could speak, a voice came to us from the inner office.

"Mr. Carter? So pleased you finally decided to join us."

"Markoski." It wasn't a question. I knew the voice.

"Very good." I heard a familiar dry chuckle. The same chuckle Markoski had given as he passed by me on his way out of the court room ten years earlier, a free man. "Why not join us, Mr. Carter?"

"Why not?" I said. "It's my office."

Jackson and I walked to my inner office and I took a careful look around the corner. Markoski was comfortably ensconced in my chair, a cigar between his lips and a mordant smile on his face. To the right of the desk was a short, pudgy man I didn't recognize, holding a snub-nose .38. Markoski saw my glance.

"My apologies," he said. "That's my right-hand man, Charles. He's the only one who has stayed faithful throughout this ordeal. He will be richly rewarded. Search them for weapons, Charles."

Charlie tried to smile pleasantly, although the attempt came off looking a lot like a shark preparing to dine upon a particularly scrumptious and unsuspecting tuna. "It has been my pleasure, sir." He approached us and removed our weapons with the dexterity of a professional.

"Indeed." After his glowing reference, Markoski seemed to immediately forget the groveling little man and turned back to me. "You have caused me no end of trouble, Mr. Carter. At first, I thought I would be satisfied with the knowledge that you were dead. Now I realize I would have been doing both of us a disservice by such a lack of attention."

"I wouldn't have been offended," I said.

Markoski laughed and it sounded so genuine that it startled me. "Amazing poise, Mr. Carter. I could have used a man like you. Sadly, it is much too late for that. Much, much too late. Ten years too late, in fact. Ever since you succeeded in having me dragged into court, I have plotted my revenge."

"You had the last word on that," I said. "Thanks to our screwed up judicial system."

"Ah, but you misunderstand the position I am in, Mr. Carter. The ignominy of being taken into a court of law was not something I should have been forced to endure. It damaged my image among the faithful and could possibly have had something to do with the disrespect and lack of loyalty I have been dealing with over the past weeks."

"Actually," I said, "I think it has more to do with the fact that you more or less abandoned your men in their hour of need. You wouldn't even pay their court costs and many of them were forced to rely on court-appointed attorneys. Then, when they finally get out, you compel them to undertake some perverse mission of personal revenge. I'd have turned on you, too."

"You always were a self-righteous son of a bitch," Markoski said without emotion. "However, your facts are somewhat erroneous. I did not force any of my men to become a part of this final mission. Those who joined did so voluntarily."

"And those who chose not to?"

Markoski smiled blandly. "There weren't many of those."

"That's because you surrounded yourself with men of reasonable intelligence," I said. "They knew it was either join you or die. Some choice."

"Your insults bore me, Mr. Carter." Markoski turned to his henchman. "Your gun, please, Charles."

The little man handed him the weapon and Markoski turned it over in his hands lovingly. He checked the load and, once satisfied the gun was in working order, pointed it at my head and sighted carefully. He held the gun there for a moment, before lowering the weapon and laughing. He was unnaturally jolly this morning and I was finding it all very disturbing.

"Pardon my little indulgences, Mr. Carter. I've waited such a long time for this moment that I can't help stretching it out a bit. Surely you don't mind?"

"Certainly not," I said. "Aim all you like. Just warn me when you decide to pull the trigger."

"You have my solemn oath." He turned to Charlie. "What can be keeping the girl?" He looked back at me and said, "I hope you don't mind me borrowing your secretary, Mr. Carter."

"Not at all. You probably had dibs on her, anyway."

"You are quite correct. I sent her your way when my plan first went into action. Her job was to keep an eye on you and report back to me regarding your whereabouts and any other unusual developments. She was also to keep you too distracted to interfere with my operation. None of the other targets received such attention. However, I have such a high regard for your resourcefulness that I felt the added precaution was warranted. Also, you were one target I had to get. You should feel flattered."

"I do, indeed. I'll add it to my résumé."

"As it turned out," Markoski said, completely ignoring my witty rejoinder, "it was well that I took such drastic measures. Without Sarah's watchful eye, I would have had no way of knowing about either Louie or Jonathon in time to stop their despicable plot. I would be a dead man, by now. And headless, if Jonathon had gotten his way." He curled a lip in revulsion. "Such brutality. Shameful."

"From what I understand, you weren't too gentle with him, either."

"He knew the risks when he crossed me," Markoski said, obviously considering himself the just party.

"Should I go check on the girl, sir?" Charlie rose from the corner of the desk where he had been sitting and looked at Markoski quizzically. "She's been gone quite awhile."

Markoski thought for a moment and nodded slowly. "Yes, do that. We can't afford any missteps at this stage in the game. But don't be long. I know you'll want to be present for the execution. Perhaps Sarah would even like to join us."

"You got it," Charlie said, giving Jackson and me a wink. He edged past us, while Markoski kept the .38 pointed our way, just in case we decided to try something stupid, a recourse I was actively considering.

Already, I had to admit to feeling rather stupid, having waltzed right into Markoski's hands. What I had expected to find when I arrived here was still unknown, but a bit more caution would definitely have been in order.

Seeming to read my mind, Markoski smiled almost sadly. "I can't help but be a little disappointed in you, Mr. Carter. Ten years ago, when you were so instrumental in toppling my empire and almost toppling me with it, I considered you a rising star in law enforcement. A definite force to be reckoned with."

"I've done alright," I said, somewhat offended by the remark, although I knew he was just needling me.

"Of course, you have," Markoski said condescendingly. "However, the ease with which I have manipulated you has both disappointed and annoyed me. I expected more of a challenge."

"It hasn't been that easy," I contradicted. "Without your little insider, you would've assumed room temperature long ago."

"Yes, but it's only by good fortune you are still here. Louie turned on me, then Jonathon. Without that, *you* would have assumed room temperature long ago."

"Then it would appear we are both the beneficiary of good fortune."

Markoski shook his head. "I disagree. A good strategist plans out several different avenues. In a chess game, one must assume the role of the opposing player and plan out their moves first, then plan strategies to counter them. They find the ideal move and plan for that, of course, but they must also guard against the possibility that their opponent will choose a less beneficial move, thereby taking them by surprise and forcing them to quickly rework their entire strategy. I am a meticulous planner, Mr. Carter, and while things may not go exactly as I originally plan them, I always have contingency plans set aside for every possibility."

"Are you saying you expected Louie and Jonny to turn on you?" I found this singularly hard to believe. "Why put them in positions to endanger you, if you didn't trust them to begin with?"

"I didn't expect them to turn on me, no. But because I was placing them in positions that made me vulnerable, I had to plan for the possibility. That's where Sarah came in."

"I thought she was to keep an eye on me."

"Ah, now that's where good fortune played a role. Yes, she was there to watch you and also Louie, since he was to be your executioner. It was, then, natural that she would know if you two met up. That was planning. I had no way of knowing, however, that Jonathon would contact you as well and that Sarah would not only answer the phone when he called, but be in the room when you carried on a less than discreet conversation. Good planning breeds good fortune."

"Planning to compose fortune cookie proverbs after this little outing?" Jackson asked, stepping forward and joining the conversation for the first time. "Because I have to tell you, what you said just got me right here."

"Interesting choice of anatomy," Markoski said, "though hardly appropriate. Your bravado is admirable, but unconvincing." He turned back to me. "Who is this gruesome gentleman?"

"Jackson Wyatt. He's a former cop who turned to fiction writing after taking a bullet in the line of duty."

"Scared you off, eh?"

"No," Jackson said. "I became a liability to the force. I had a lot of physical therapy and doctor bills after the incident and the department decided I'd be too much bother, so they bought me out." He smiled at Markoski. "I barely missed being involved in your meltdown. Just think, I could have been on the lists, too."

"For all intents and purposes, you are, Mr. Wyatt. I certainly cannot let you go, since you have witnessed these proceedings." He scowled. "Where is that fool Charles? Impossible to get good help these days."

I snorted. "Tell me about it."

"Charles!"

There was no answer, of course. Charlie was not in the office and certainly wouldn't hear his name being called from anywhere else in the building.

My cell phone rang and I looked at Markoski. "May I?"

"Certainly. But do it slowly."

I did so and the deliberative manner helped me hide my surprise when I saw who was calling.

"Hello?"

"Kirk." Sarah's voice was not at all sheepish, as well it should have been considering the circumstances.

"Yes, ma'am," I responded, not wanting Markoski to know who I was talking to. "What can I do for you, Mrs. Chandler?"

Sarah giggled in a very non-ruthless manner. "The only reason I'll let you get away with that is because I know why you did it. I understand the old man has you at gun point."

"Quite."

"You may want to find a way around that within the next ten minutes or so."

"Meaning?"

"Simply this. Charlie and I aren't coming back. It was all planned. I'd stay gone until Markoski sent him to look for me. We'd meet up and scram. Charlie has been Markoski's right-hand man for some time, now, and knows where the money is and has access to it."

"Why ten minutes?"

"That's when the bomb will go off."

"Come again?"

"It's to kill Markoski. That's been the plan all along."

"You were in it with Louie and Jonny?"

"Bingo. But we couldn't get him into the open and then my partners started dropping like flies. Before long, there was only Charlie and me left and we knew Markoski would probably take the matter into his own hands, which would mean leaving his lair long enough to be neatly disposed of."

"Why are you doing this?"

There was a moment of silence and when she spoke again, Sarah's voice portrayed a woman scorned. "Charlie told me about Markoski's plan to leave the country once all the killings were completed. He was planning to start fresh, which meant I wasn't going. I may have been just his mistress, but I took the idea personally. I felt that was a good enough reason. That and the money, of course."

"Oh, of course." I glanced toward Markoski, who was looking at me strangely. "Why are you telling me this? I would think you'd want me out of the way."

"That was in the original plan, but Charlie and I have nothing against you, really. We decided killing Markoski and letting you go would be a final, bitter irony."

"Aren't you afraid I'll track you down if you let me live?"

"Why should you? I've done nothing to harm you, have I? And look at your office files. I even finished that job before I left."

I took a look around the office. It was true. Everything was neatly arranged and organized. The filing cabinets were immaculate, the drawers carefully labeled.

"Nicely done," I said, "but I was thinking more along the lines of Leslie. He died, you know. I take that rather personal."

"And so you should." Sarah's voice softened a bit. "You may not believe me, but I did not plan his death or even know it was to take place. I didn't hear about the plan until it was too late." There was a pause and then she said, "I would have warned him, you know. I actually did like him. There was a mutual attraction. I didn't lie about that."

"Such scruples," I said sarcastically. "Where is the...item?"

"Under the desk. Where Markoski is sitting. It's not exactly the A-bomb, but you'll want to at least be out of the inner office. Nick and I planted it yesterday while you and Jackson were out running around."

"Didn't it strike you as odd that Leslie never showed up for work? Nick was involved in his killing, didn't he mention anything about that?"

"No, I swear I knew nothing about it. I was here all day to make sure Nick could get in with the equipment. We set up the bomb and had some materials remaining, so Nick stored the leftovers in the trunk of his car. Then he drove me back to my hotel room."

Leftover materials in Gantry's trunk. No wonder the blast at the parking ramp had seemed so powerful. It hadn't been just gasoline, after all.

"You don't really expect me to just let this happen, do you?"

"Kirk, the man's a killer. Let it go. The bomb's rigged to be remotely detonated and my finger's on the button. Get out of the office."

"I can't let you do this."

"You can't stop me, Kirk. You've been warned. I'm sorry."

"Wait!"

"I'll wait a few seconds to let you get out of the office and then I'm pulling the trigger on this thing. You can get out, but Markoski's too lame to move quickly. Don't make me kill you."

She hung up, but I continued to hold the phone to my ear for just a moment after the connection ended. Then I shook myself from my stupor.

I stepped forward, but Markoski held the gun toward me and I saw the knuckle of his trigger finger whiten as he began squeezing.

"Hold it right there, Mr. Carter. Not a step closer."

"Markoski, that was Sarah on the phone. She says there's a bomb under the desk. It's rigged to go off via remote detonation and she's got the controls. We only have a few seconds."

Markoski looked at me strangely and then laughed. "Now that is just pitiful," he said. "Surely you can come up with something better than that."

"I could," I said, "but I don't need to when I'm telling you the truth. If you'll just look under the desk, you'll see that's exactly what I'm doing."

"And give you the opportunity to jump me? You must think me a fool. Don't insult me, Mr. Carter."

"Insult you! I'm trying to save your life, dammit!"

"Another reason why this is such a ridiculous ruse," Markoski said. "Why would you want to save my life? Even you aren't that noble, Mr. Carter."

I knew Sarah was probably pressing the button at that very moment, so I did the only thing I could think of. I screamed my head off and chucked the cell phone right at Markoski's grinning face. The device caught him squarely between the eyes and he jerked back, first instinctively at my sudden outburst and then in pain as the blow opened a cut on his forehead. The .38

barked and I felt a sting as a bullet went through my hair and grazed the scalp. At the same moment, I dropped to the floor and rolled out of the office, with Jackson right behind me.

The last thing I saw as I tumbled into the main office was Markoski, his face a mask of fury and terror as he realized I had been telling the truth, struggling to pull himself out of the chair and come around the desk. He never made it.

There was a tremendous roar and a billowing cloud of red-laced smoke blew out the door to the inner office. The windows in the office shattered and I felt the floor tremble beneath me.

I crawled through the smoke, dust, and debris and peered into what had been my personal office just a few seconds before. The desk was completely shattered and the walls were ravaged and burnt. Markoski was lying in a corner. At least, half of him was. The other half was nowhere to be seen, except for one shoe, which was lodged behind a hideously melted plastic fern.

Jackson coughed and crawled up behind me. "You're dangerous company," he wheezed, the smoke and dust clogging his lungs. "That's the third time in two days I've almost died, just because I was near you. I'm thinking this little vacation of mine may not have been the best idea. I don't feel at all rested."

"You know you love the attention," I said, as the building's fire alarms began wailing. "Besides, I'm going to need somebody to help put this office back together. Crap! Sarah just got my office in order and then she promptly blows it up. Personally, I consider that highly unproductive."

Jackson peered into the office and burst out laughing. I consider myself just as willing to enjoy humor as the next guy, but I must confess that I found Jackson's jocularity somewhat inappropriate.

"What the hell is so funny?" I asked irritably. "This is not the time for your morbid humor."

Still laughing and unable to speak, Jackson simply pointed at the object of his mirth. I followed his point and, at first, saw nothing to elicit even a chuckle. Then I saw them. The huge, metal filing cabinets had barely even been scratched. Sarah's handiwork was safe.

Epilogue

I tossed the teddy bear like a football and Derrick caught it expertly. Not a bad catch, considering the little guy was still bound to the hospital bed. Of course, it had also been an expert throw.

Mrs. Bertram and Bob Croswell were both all smiles. The doctors had proclaimed Derrick out of danger the night of the gala and he was already showing marked improvement.

"Kids bounce back like jumping beans," Croswell said, reaching down to mess the boy's hair. "He'll be out playing football again before we know it."

Derrick looked up at me eagerly. "Will you play football with me, Mr. Carter?"

"I'd love to," I said, but Jackson moved up beside me and shook his head gravely.

"I wouldn't advise that, Derrick. Kirk's a pretty lousy football player. Every time he throws it looks like he's trying to fend off a swarm of bats."

"What are you saying?" I turned to him in disgust. "Didn't you just see that throw with the teddy bear? It was beautiful!"

"Yeah, for the other team. That would have been an interception for sure."

I had some choice words for Jackson, but there were children in the room. He was one of them. Instead, I leaned over and shook Derrick's hand.

"Glad you're feeling better, buddy. We'll play soon."

As Jackson and I left the hospital room, I punched him in the arm, intending to inflict pain. He yelped and grabbed the injured arm in a gratifying manner.

"Who are you to criticize my football prowess?"

Jackson laughed. "I know I'm cruel, but I just like kicking people when they're down."

"Beg pardon?"

"You. Don't tell me it hasn't yet occurred to you that you might be losing your touch."

"I still don't get you."

"Sarah. Come on, Kirk. You've always prided yourself on being a hand with the ladies, but you ended up losing a dish like Sarah to a lout like Charlie. I'd take that personally, if I were you."

"I didn't lose Sarah to Charlie," I said patiently, although Jackson was right. The thought had occurred to me. "I lost her to Markoski's money. If it hadn't been for that, she'd be under my spell at this very moment."

"So you're not worried about your waning ability to woo the ladies?"

"Now you're just being an idiot. I've never been more viral in my life."

To prove my point, I smiled at a passing nurse and nearly killed myself by tripping over a food cart some thoughtless orderly had left in the hallway.

"Easy, Romeo," Jackson said, not even trying to smother his laughter. "You don't have to prove anything to me." He became serious. "All joking aside, Kirk, how are you doing? You've taken a lot of crap over the past few days."

I shrugged. "I'd be lying if I said I was fine, but I'll survive. The biggest challenge is going to be putting the business back together after the explosion and the loss of Leslie. We had a pretty heavy caseload."

"I could help."

The offer came out of nowhere and brought me to a halt. "Are you serious?"

Jackson nodded. "Absolutely. I've had some rough spots in my writing lately and perhaps a change of scenery would stir my creative juices. Maybe I just need a distraction. Plus, working with an actual PI will help in my research. I write mysteries, you know."

"Yeah, I actually managed to read a couple," I said. "Seriously, they were pretty good. Do you think you could fill Leslie's shoes?"

"No," Jackson said. "Honestly, I'm not sure how much help I would be. But I'd love to give it a shot."

"Consider yourself hired."

Actually, the offer was a welcome development. I had spent the entire previous night wondering how I would make it through the next few days. My spirits raised a little and, acting purely on habit, I reached into my side pocket for a celebratory cigarette.

Jackson saw my movement and knew what I was searching for. He shook his head and gave me a disapproving look. I sighed and withdrew a piece of Nicorette from my shirt pocket. I put the gum in my mouth and chewed. I looked at Jackson and raised a questioning eyebrow, as if to say, "Happy now?"

He smiled and nodded. Perhaps Jackson would be able to fill Leslie's shoes after all.

THE END

Also by Craig Alan Hart

The Ballad of Duke Dookums

The Wild West will never be the same with Duke Dookums, Frontier Hero on the job. Outlaws, villains, and other unpleasant characters know and fear him.

Trouble seems to follow Duke as he rides through the lawless expanse of the frontier, but our intrepid hero is more than up to the task.

This lively kids' book is sure to delight and entertain children of all ages. Join Duke as he takes on the nastiest bad guys the West has to offer.

Paperback 978-0615139777

Pick up your copy today!
Sweatshoppe Publications
Grand Rapids, Michigan